ALL THINGS
Beautiful

PATRICE JOSEPH

Trilogy Christian Publishers
A Wholly Owned Subsidiary of Trinity Broadcasting Network
2442 Michelle Drive
Tustin, CA 92780
Copyright © 2024 by Patrice Joseph
Scripture quotations marked NLT are taken from the Holy Bible, New Living Translation, copyright © 1996, 2004, 2015 by Tyndale House Foundation. Used by permission of Tyndale House Publishers, Inc., Carol Stream, Illinois 60188. All rights reserved.
All rights reserved, including the right to reproduce this book or portions thereof in any form whatsoever.
For information, address Trilogy Christian Publishing
Rights Department, 2442 Michelle Drive, Tustin, Ca 92780.
Trilogy Christian Publishing/ TBN and colophon are trademarks of Trinity Broadcasting Network.
For information about special discounts for bulk purchases, please contact Trilogy Christian Publishing.

Trilogy Disclaimer: The views and content expressed in this book are those of the author and may not necessarily reflect the views and doctrine of Trilogy Christian Publishing or the Trinity Broadcasting Network.

10 9 8 7 6 5 4 3 2 1
Library of Congress Cataloging-in-Publication Data is available.
ISBN 979-8-89333-794-5
ISBN 979-8-89333-793-8 (ebook)

DEDICATION

To my mom, who has always been my number one fan. I love you.

To the people who have given up reading fiction in pursuit of the Lord, I hope this gives you all the vibes and feels.

To my younger self, who always wanted to be a storyteller, you are living your wildest dreams. Even if they are happening in slow motion.

"We are writing these things so that you may fully share our joy" (1 John 1:4, NLT).

TABLE OF CONTENTS

Prologue 9
Chapter 1 27
Chapter 2 41
Chapter 3 55
Chapter 4 67
Chapter 5 77
Chapter 6 93
Chapter 7 105
Chapter 8 121
Chapter 9 137
Chapter 10 155
Chapter 11 171
Chapter 12 189
Chapter 13 201
Chapter 14 209
Chapter 15 221
Chapter 16 235
Chapter 17 249
Epilogue 261

PROLOGUE

Winter

I swore girls had cooties until I met her.

"Are you coming or not?" she asked, only looking over her shoulder once before taking heavy strides up the snow-peaked hill.

I glanced quickly at my older brother, Eden, not sure if I should let him know I was leaving with a stranger. A girl I had only just met. A girl who looked like the hottest day of winter, if that makes any sense at all.

Although I could only barely make out her figure getting lost beneath the hill, I decided against my instincts and let Eden know I was leaving. Just in case.

"Hey, I'm going on the ski lift with a…friend." Yeah, I think she's my friend, but I also don't want to get ahead of myself.

I looked at Eden and the band of misfits he often attracted, regardless of where our parents wanted to vacation. I watched as he rolled up the greenery in a brownish paper and sealed the ends with a lick of his tongue.

"Eden?" I voice again, unsure he'd heard me the first

time.

"Got it, Z. You could've just texted me, bro. I'm not your keeper," Eden retorted with a scowl, causing his friends to laugh and give me estranged looks.

I was used to him making me feel small or insignificant, and while I typically would've countered him, today, it didn't matter.

I raised the hem of my Himalayan suit, took the fastest steps I could in my heavy boots, and ran until I finally caught up to where she stood in line.

"Excuse me," I huffed, nearly bent over in an attempt to catch my breath. "I'm with her." I apologized to the people behind me and stood beside the girl with no name.

She had a beautiful, deep brown complexion that, even in the snow, beamed hints of pure gold. Her hair, though tucked underneath a protective cap, was curly and brown from the one piece that kept falling onto her face. I watched as her honey-brown eyes scanned me, and the corners of her mouth turned up into a smile. Was she also happy that I caught up to her in time?

"Took you long enough." She smirked before laughing.

***

"You haven't done this before, have you?" She raised her eyebrow and looked at me.

I swallowed down the lump in my throat. She was the one person in the world that I wanted to think of me as brave.

"I have," I lied. "I just get a little jittery each time. But I'm good."

She squinted her eyes at me as if she could see right through me and knew I was lying.

"How old are you?" she asked.

"Twelve. How about you?"

"I'm twelve, too. Okay, now it's your turn to ask me a question."

"Is this a game?"

"Well, not really…but I can tell you're nervous. My dad and I always try new things together. He says I'm a dare devil like my mom…" She chewed the corner of her lip. "Anyhow, if I'm ever nervous, he makes me talk and laugh. He says it's the best cure for nerves."

"Oh…okay." I tried not to dwell too much on the fact that she already considered me to be a scared little kid when she was obviously much more adventurous than me, but at least I could get to know her. And that would be a small victory of its own. "What's your favorite color?" I questioned back.

"Black. Yours?"

"Blue."

She let out a breath and rolled her eyes, "How ubiquitous of you. All boys say that their favorite color is blue…boring."

"How so?" I asked, slightly offended.

"Ubiquitous basically means—"

"No," I interrupted. "I know what the word means. I just didn't think blue was that popular of a color."

She shrugged. "Well, it's a common color for boys. At least where I'm from," she responded matter-of-factly. "What city do you live in? Assuming that you're also here on vacation."

"Yeah. We are. My family and I live in Charleston."

"South Carolina or West Virginia?" she posed.

I laughed, "So you're going to question all of my answers this whole game, huh?"

"Only if your answers aren't coherent." She smiled, sending a pulse of what I could only explain as electricity to my chest.

"South Carolina."

"Hmmm…. Old money, I see."

I shook my head and shrugged my shoulders. "What

about you? Where do you and your family live?"

For a brief moment, her smile flinched. "It's just me and my dad." She puffed out her chest a bit, assuredly. "He's my best friend, and I'm his. We just moved to Atlanta."

"New money, I see."

She laughed so hard that the chair beneath us rocked, reminding me we were suspended about thirty feet above the ground. She grabbed my hand and the railing started to lift, signaling we'd be expected to get off soon.

"I've done this a million times before with my dad. We can jump together."

I nodded my head, afraid that if I opened my mouth, she'd be covered in my breakfast.

"What's your name?" I managed to ask. If I die here, I at least want to lie in eternal rest, having known her name.

"Okay, it's almost on us. Slide forward in your chair and point your skis upward like this." She motioned how she wanted me to follow her directions, and I complied. "Once your skis are touching the ground completely, just stand up; you don't really jump."

"Oh. Okay, I didn't know that." I let out a breath of relief.

She smirked. "I knew you never did this before."

I stared down at our interlocked hands. Even though we both had on gloves her touch was that of fire. And for her, I would burn.

Spring

"C'mon, Dad, the line is becoming absurd." I tugged at my dad's arm, not caring if I was interrupting his work call.

He pulled the receiver away from his ear and sighed. "This one might be a minute, baby girl. How about you get on the Ferris wheel in the meantime, and when you're done, we'll ride the roller coaster together."

I sucked my teeth, "The Ferris wheel, Dad? Really? That's for babies and lovebirds."

We negotiated a deal, as we usually did when we disagreed, and I made my way to the Ferris wheel line, determined to skip as many families as possible to make my way to the front quickly. Most of the families and couples didn't notice as I snaked my way around them until someone tapped my shoulder.

"Hey, uhhh…I think you dropped your tickets."

"Oh…no, these aren't mine. I have a pass…" I turned around and got a glimpse of a familiar pair of hazel eyes, even though I couldn't quite register a face.

He picked up the scattered tickets from the floor and

stacked them into a neat, meticulous pile before handing them over to me.

"Do you want them anyway? You never know." He shrugged, still not looking at me directly.

"No. Today's my last day here."

He handed the tickets to a little girl and her brother twirling around each other who were standing behind me. The girl shrieked and thanked him, and the boy fist-bumped the air in excitement. He chuckled before looking at me directly and smiling the widest smile I'd ever seen a guy give me.

"Hey, I know you…um…. It's New Money, right?"

"Hey! Oh wow…" An unexpected warmth shimmied its way to my face. "Are you and your family here on vacation?"

He answered, his eyes never leaving mine. But each time he blinked, I found myself stealing glimpses of his face and body. His skin and freckles were both various sandy shades of brown. He'd grown out his hair a bit, and black locs tickled his strong jaw line. And that jaw had small patches of peach fuzz growing in. His body had filled out from when I last saw him, and soft muscles peaked beneath his shirt.

"…but yeah. That's us. How about you?"

"Umm…" I blew a breath out between my pursed lips. "I'm sorry I missed your question."

"Are you also here with your family?"

"Oh yeah. It's just me and my dad." I raised my hand to block out the sun from my eyes and looked over to the bench where my father was sitting. His phone call had ended, and he was watching my interaction with this guy I kind of but don't really know.

I gestured for him to come over and join me, but he smiled and waved me off.

It was always just me and my dad, and I liked it that way. I had heard people say I would grow out of being best friends with my father, but as I aged, our relationship aged, and our bond only became stronger.

I shifted my hand over my eye and smiled back widely at my father.

***

"If you're not good with heights, why do you keep doing this to yourself?" I continued to rub the back of my now hunched-over, still unfamiliar friend.

We were in our clear-view Ferris wheel cabin and had just made it to the stop at the top. The view was breathtaking to me, but the sight only made him want to puke.

He lifted his face and looked at me with a look of curiosity and finality, making me feel abnormally nervous.

"Honestly speaking, I wasn't really in line. I thought you were a stranger who dropped your tickets, and when I realized it was *you*, I had to talk to you longer."

His freckled features turned up into a cheeky smile, and I looked out the window to hide my now-heated face. I tried to push the feelings and my warming face down with a gulp.

"Can you do that thing again…? Your secret cure for nerves." He wiped the small beads of sweat from his forehead with the back of his hand.

"Oh, you remember that?" I laughed, my own nervousness now leaving my body. "Well, I'm sixteen now, so you must be sixteen, too, right?"

"Yeah, I am. When's your birthday?" he returned.

"August 15th. Yours?"

His eyebrows lifted. "August 15th, believe it or not."

"Well, statistically speaking, 15 million people celebrate a birthday every day. And on average, more people are born in the month of August than in any other month. About 9 percent more, if I recall. So, not the weirdest thing."

"I remember that, too." He shook his head and smiled again.

"Oh." This is why I don't have any other real friends besides my dad. "I'm too smart for my own good, with a smart mouth to match," is what my grandmother used to say. I can't help it. I am used to it though, and I've grown to be acquainted and fond of the silence in loneliness.

"I didn't know that about birthdays. That's actually cool that you knew that. I'm not that big into numbers."

"I wouldn't say I'm big into math, although I am quite good at it. My favorite subjects are a tie between biology and chemistry. But that's school. Art is my favorite subject in life. What are yours?"

"School or life?" he asked.

"Both."

"I am really interested in history and English. And life?" He stared out the glass and looked towards the sky. "I guess I would say people and finding out the answers to questions such as why we're here, you know?"

"You're interesting." I slid back into the chair until my back was straight against the see-through wall behind me.

He mimicked my posture and looked at me with those hazel eyes that, in this lighting, revealed specks of green.

"I accept that compliment coming from you because I think you're the most fascinating person I've ever met."

I smirked. "What makes you say that?"

"I don't have one straight answer, but that doesn't make it any less true."

"Hmm."

We sat in silence for a moment and stared at each other. And what started out feeling like an awkward blinking contest drifted into a recognizable peace.

"Are you ever going to tell me your name?"

"And ruin all of this mystery that makes me fascinating? Most certainly not."

He threw his head back and let out a laugh that both startled and comforted me. "I like you, New."

"I think I like you too, Old."

Summer

"Come on. Let's pray again. God will hear us." My teary mother sniffled as she grabbed my hand, and both she and my father started praying for my older brother Eden.

Over the years, my brother's bad habits trailed slowly into addictions. Sometimes, we went weeks looking for him, only for him to drop in after a bender. I had to cover for him too many times to count when he was secretly high in his room because I couldn't bear to break my mother's heart with the truth. While she and my father had a limitless amount of grace and forgiveness towards him, I personally had grown tired of picking up the pieces after his cyclical storms had passed. Today, his blood alcohol levels were in the four hundreds, the test showed, and while he was incoherent, having tremors, and defecating on himself... my parents were here, praying for him.

"I'll be right back, guys. You both pray. I need to get some air." I gently dropped my mother's hand and rushed towards the exit while she and my father continued to travail in prayer.

I made my way toward the waiting room and hung my head with feelings of exhaustion coursing through my neck and shoulders. I took my last final of the semester today before flying home, and I'd been studying nearly twelve hours a day for the past week. The last thing I needed right now was to be here.

I pulled out my phone and thumbed through my text messages.

Two years since reconnecting with her at a fair in Myrtle Beach, I still didn't know her name, but I knew her in all the ways that mattered. We communicated just about every day. We wished each other mutual happy birthdays, sent random pictures of ourselves throughout the day, and talked about almost everything. Even though we were both now in different colleges hundreds of miles apart, she had grown to know me in a way I didn't think was possible. It was always obvious when one of us was dating someone, although it remained unsaid because the frequency of our communication would all but stop. However, nothing ever stuck; no one compared to her, at least not to me.

I started to text her when a message popped through on my phone.

> New Money: I was going to surprise you by letting you know I was in your city. But don't think I'll be able to see you. My dad's in the hospital... He's all good, just a bad headache, but still.

I rose to my feet and immediately FaceTimed her. While waiting for her, I started pacing the hallways of the emergency room at Charleston Regional Medical Center. I called her three times back to back before she answered.

"Hey, sorry. I was talking to the nurse, looking for the waiting room." She looked down at her phone and noticed I was also in the hospital. "Are you in Charleston Regional…?"

I was too busy staring at the face of the most beautiful woman I'd ever met before to notice I had completely walked straight into someone.

"I am so sorry about this," I stammered. "Truly." I reached down to pick up the Ninja Turtle-designed key ring, a small wallet, and raspberry lip gloss.

"You know, we have got to stop meeting like this." She laughed and reached her hand over to take her keys from my hand.

Perhaps it was because I wasn't expecting to see her. Perhaps it was the exhaustion I was feeling that had weakened my inhibitions and usual strong will and self-control. Perhaps it was fate and God's timing, like my dad would say, but seeing her face to face again after two years of failed meetups, I wrapped my arms around her and pulled her into myself.

I could feel her tension fade away as she started to hug me back. Her hair was tucked in a bun that sat right underneath my nose, allowing me to take in her fresh scent mixed with hints of vanilla and argan oil.

With her arms still wrapped around me, she peered up and looked at me with those same honey-brown eyes that have haunted and graced my dreams for years. She could ask for my whole heart right now, and I would give it to her. No questions asked. She chewed on the corner of her lip. I have come to know her well enough to know that meant she was nervous. I bent my head down and kissed her. Her lips were soft, her movements were subtle but captivating, and her mouth tasted like raspberries.

After sharing our first kiss, we walked together, hand in hand, towards her father's hospital room while I envisioned the rest of our lives together.

"You're going to fly three times a semester from Yale to Stanford to visit me? On your work-study paycheck? Yeah, right." She laughed. "We can take turns visiting each other once a semester. We've made it this long."

She continued to look between me and her sleeping father. Her smile never fading since we kissed and decided to make things official between us. She has no clue that I'll be running on empty once she leaves until I see her again.

"Baby girl, you're not going to let me get any rest, huh?" Her father croaked weakly from his bed.

She rose up from her seat and nearly skipped over towards her father. She wrapped her arms around him and kissed his cheek before formally introducing us. We had spoken briefly several times over the last two years. He referred to me as "Young Man" since New Money was strict about us not exchanging names for whatever reason. Their relationship was open, honest, and free, in a way I hadn't experienced or seen with any of my friends and their parents.

We spent a few minutes talking together, and every so often, I would catch him looking at her and smiling in a way that seemed so proud. He warned me to treat her well but also said he had a really good feeling about me and that his feelings were never wrong.

I pulled out my phone and noticed my mom was calling. I spoke to her briefly and let her know I would be on my way shortly.

"We should exchange names now, huh? Since you're my boyfriend?"

"That we should." I could soar at the realization that, finally, we were together, and not just in the way before, but in a way that meant more than just long calls and endless messages. In a way that felt tangible. In a way cemented by words.

"Okay, let me guess…" She ran her fingers through my locs before stepping back and looking at me. She grabbed my chin and angled it in the same way I'd seen her move and mold around clay or whatever she was working on numerous times during our video calls.

"You're never going to guess; people always say it's unique."

"People say the same about me, right, Dad?"

She looked over to her father and let out a loud, guttural scream. One that I was sure would stay with me throughout the course of my life.

From what I can remember, and from the limited medical knowledge I know now, her father had died from a ruptured brain aneurysm.

Before I knew it, the room was rushed with medical professionals, and since I wasn't family, I had to leave the room.

I tried calling, but no answer. I texted, nothing. Not even on our birthday. I kept that up for years before deciding it was time to move on with my life. If you can call what I did moving on.

The plans and dreams I hoped would come to fruition died before one of them began.

CHAPTER 1

Autumn

"Mooooom! It's the first day of school. Must we be late on the first day?" My eleven-year-old daughter, Peyton, complained.

Peyton threw herself over my lap while I laced up my sneakers. She plucked at the bright orange laces and audibly pouted.

"Mom. It's the first day. Would it absolutely kill you to give a little more vogue?" She rolled off my lap onto the floor and crisscrossed her legs.

I grabbed her face and kissed her cheek. "It would *absolutely* kill me."

Despite my natural tomboyishness, Peyton came out of me with a bejeweled crown, pink lipgloss, and sass. I loved every bit of her ferociously, and while I often let her dress me up, today wasn't a day for pomp and pumps.

She threw her head back and lifted both hands in defeat. "Fine, Mom. I don't have time to deal with this today.

But can we please leave now? I want to make a great first impression." She grabbed my hands and pulled on them until I was standing on my feet. "Let's get to it, ma'am."

Our relationship was unorthodox, sure. Still, it was ours. Peyton was truly my little best friend. I thoroughly enjoyed her company as much as I enjoyed being with my dad for all the years that I had him.

I ran my fingers through her freshly straightened hair. Looking at her was literally looking at my mirror. Only it didn't reflect me now, but a younger, lighter me.

I shimmy my shoulders and will myself not to linger on thoughts of my father. While remembering him didn't always lead me to uncontrollable tears, it always led me to miss him. Both left me feeling empty and still. I had time for neither today.

"Okay, Sweet P. Let's go."

We screeched songs together in perfect disharmony the entire car ride to her new school.

As I looked at her in between song hooks we loved, I thought back to Peyton's first day of school when she was two and in daycare. She cried until she completely tired herself out and fell asleep for a week straight. Her preschool teacher encouraged me that this was normal and she would eventually get used to a new routine. I kept trying to push down my mom guilt, but I just couldn't. I thought of all the memories I treasured with my father and decided to homeschool her. When she turned seven, we packed our bags and traveled the world together. I savored every moment of our very own eat, pray, love.

After her studies, we'd swim with dolphins, mountain bike, and do whatever else to our hearts' content, depending on what region of the world we were in. I added to the album of memories I shared during travels with my dad. For me, that was enough.

One day after watching a movie as our typical Friday night ritual, she decided she needed "more social interaction with human beings her own age." Her words, not mine. Together, we picked a city and a school and moved. She was growing up, and I couldn't be her whole world anymore, regardless of how much I'd miss her.

Peyton turned the dial on the volume and faced me, chewing on the corner of her lip. "Mommy, do you think they'll like me? And don't give me the parental figure answer. Give it to me straight."

"Okay, straight up, no chaser. You're the most amazing person I know in the whole entire world, period. You're going to do so well, I am sure of it. Just…just try not to therapize anyone. At least not on the first day."

She rolled her eyes, blew raspberries, and rested the back of her hand on her forehead dramatically. "No way, Mom. I won't be open for sessions until at least a week into school. I need to scope out the social environment first. Then, I'll make an impact."

I nudged her side and laughed. "Okay, dude. Have a great day."

We kissed each other goodbye. She unfastened her seatbelt and hopped out of my car. Once on the sidewalk near the school entrance, she did a final spin, showing off her outfit. She added pink and yellow laces and socks, pink barrettes in her hair, and sewed a pink and gold letter P to her skirt. She insisted she needed to have full autonomy over her creative expression of self, and that wearing the uniform the regular way deprived her of the right. Again, her words. Of course, as luck would have it, she inherited my smart mouth.

"You too, Mom. I'm praying you have a great day and don't miss me too much. But text me if you do. Oh, and make sure to keep a mental note of everything, and we'll swap stories after school. Love you. Bye." She smiled and waved before hopping away.

"God." I sighed. "Please keep my baby safe."

***

"Z, I owe you one."

"No! Don't worry about it. I was committed to the idea that I'd be spending the day staring at the walls until Peyton got out of school. Believe me, I'm happy to be getting out of the house."

Nicole continued to thank me for helping her.

When we moved into our new home here in Atlanta, Peyton all but physically forced me to introduce ourselves to our neighbors. She said I also needed social interaction with peers my own age. Everyone was kind enough, but Nicole was genuinely friendly and welcoming. She invited Peyton and me over to dinner that same day. Nicole was not only a former ballerina dancer who ran an after-school program, but she was also an amazing home chef. We did dinners together at least once a week, and although I'd only known her for a few weeks, she was the closest thing to friendship I'd experienced with anyone who wasn't blood. At least for a long time now.

"Yeah, but still. I'll make you the banana pudding again. I know how much you loved that last week."

"Now, *that* I'll actually take you up on." I pointed at her, and we shared a laugh.

Her phone chimed and she responded back to a text message. "My brother-in-law is here with his girls. I'm going to get them, and then we'll take attendance and get started."

Nicole started an after-school program that helped children in elementary school with homework while also

ALL THINGS BEAUTIFUL

introducing them to sports, dance, art, theater, and music. Last minute, her art teacher dropped out, and she asked if I would fill in until she found a permanent replacement.

Nicole walked back in with the cutest set of twins. They sat on the bleachers with the other children.

"Okay, everyone! Welcome to this year's first day of REACH! I'm so happy to have you all. It's not too many new faces here so you guys know the drill. Get in the line of what subject you'd like to learn this week and then we can get started!" Nicole cheered into the microphone.

After a round of applause, introductions from the teachers, and a few other announcements, the students got up and into lines. In the art line were five children. Three boys and two girls, including the twins Nicole had walked in with.

After the homework session ended, I tied smocks around each of the little artists. I didn't expect to enjoy teaching little ones about brush techniques and color theory. I'm sure most of what I said today went over their heads, but it was still exhilarating watching them create their own ideas of beauty on canvas.

By 4 p.m., most of the kids had been picked up by their parents. Hope and Grace, the twins, both decided to sit in with me and help me put the canvases in a safe place to dry.

"Thank you both so much for helping. I think we're all

done." I squatted down onto my knees to get eye level with both girls.

"You're welcome, Ms. Z." Hope smiled, showing her missing two front teeth.

"Ms. Z, you're so pretty." Grace smiled.

"Oh, thank you sooo much, Grace. You're the pretty one. Both of you are." I shifted glances between the two.

Grace and Hope were both five years old and in kindergarten. They each had a set of familiar hazel eyes and brown sandy freckles. Both of them had a reddish brown hair color, although Hope's hair was a loose curl pattern, and Grace had tighter kinks and coils.

We continued to talk, and I realized these two were the most polite set of girls I'd ever met. They continued to compliment me on how the class went, how fun it was to paint and get messy, my sneakers, and even my hair.

"All right, girls. It's time for us to get out of here. Everyone else is gone." Nicole came in, and the girls ran to her and hugged her.

"Again, thank you so much for helping out today. I have posts on LinkedIn and Indeed. I just need a few more days, two weeks max, if that's okay?" Nicole asked, holding a niece in each hand.

"It wasn't too bad. Honestly, I had a good time. And

these two were star students." I gave each girl a thumbs-up, and they giggled and returned the gesture.

Nicole trumpeted, "So does this mean you're going to join #TeamREACH?"

I buried both hands into my pockets while flexing and arching my feet on the pavement. "Can I get back to you on that?"

"Oh my gosh. Yes. Absolutely! No pressure, but if you want to be here, we'd love to have you."

"I'll think it over and let you know soon, though, okay?"

"Sure. Whatever you decide, it'll work out for the good."

***

"Cheers, Mommy!" Peyton lifted her champagne flute filled with sparkling cider.

"Cheers, Sweet P!" I clinked her cider flute with my wine glass.

We finished dinner and Peyton suggested we'd celebrate an eventful first day.

"I really thought I was going to come home and find you curled up in a corner counting sheep," she remarked. "But I'm so proud of you for stepping out of your comfort zone and having an amazing day."

"Am I the parent here, or is it you? Please remind me."

"Today it's you. But it'll probably be me again tomorrow." Peyton laughed before taking a sip out of her flute and setting it down on the coffee table. "I will say, though, I'd be even more impressed if your day included more adult communication."

She lay on the couch and propped her feet in my lap, "But baby steps. This is still progress."

"Peyton, please. I can't deal with one of your sessions tonight."

Peyton and I had binged a few seasons of *Iyanla: Fix My Life* while snowed in during a winter storm in Montreal. Since then, she has read a few different applied psychology books and rededicated her life to counseling. However, she was still going to be a chic therapist who sits front row during New York Fashion Week. Again, her words.

"Okay, but I just want you to know that you're deflecting. Tell me more about your day."

"Well, that's it. Lunch with Nicole, then class, and yeah, the two most well-mannered girls in the world. I have no clue where I went wrong with you." I swatted her feet, and we shared a laugh.

"You know it would be nice to have a little sister. She would look up to me and listen to me. And you know I give the best advice." Peyton peeked up at me over her cellphone.

"I'll keep that in mind for my next trip to the sperm bank."

"Mom, don't be gross! We literally just ate. But maybe we can adopt or something? It's the twenty-first century; we have options."

"This seems like something you've thought about before."

"Well. That's because it is. We make a great team, Mom. I feel in my heart we have so much more love to give." Peyton cupped both of her hands over the middle of her chest.

"*We*, huh?"

"Well…you wouldn't need my help if you would go out on a date." Peyton sat up and crawled closer to me. "You're a baddie, Mom. Trust me on this. You could get a date if you wanted one."

I took a large gulp of my wine. I hadn't been on a real date in years. I downloaded a few dating apps maybe once every six months and was always quickly reminded of why I was single. It's not that there weren't attractive men, it's not even that I didn't get asked out every now and again, but when you meet someone who makes you belly laugh and is able to hold a stimulating conversation…everyone else dulls in comparison.

After swallowing down a gulp that consisted of what ifs and regret, I continued, "Anyhow, enough about me. Tell me more about your day."

"I'm going to have a lot of business. That's a fact. I counted at least thirteen tragic cases today. Most of my classes are a yawn; this year is going to be a breeze."

"Well, first, that's because you have a genius for a mom. And secondly, please, please, please do not charge these people's kids for services. You are not a licensed therapist, miss ma'am."

"Not *yet.*" Peyton let out an exasperated sigh. "Mom, I'm not doing this for money. I'm really passionate about helping people. And besides, as long as you're still giving me allowance, I don't need to charge them."

"Mm-hmm." I continued to sip my glass of Pinot and motioned for her to continue.

"Most of my teachers are either apathetic or boring. I know I'm going to have to do my own readings to really learn anything. But Mom! My English teacher, Mr. Timothy? I already love his class. Once he figured out I had read most of the books in the syllabus, he created a new list for me featuring a bunch of black, brown, and female authors. Just for me, Mom."

She continued to rant and rave about her new school and her teachers.

ALL THINGS BEAUTIFUL

"It sounds like you had a really good day. I'm happy you like your new school, babe."

We finished our drinks, caught up on our shows, and got ready for bed. Tonight, like many nights, she fell asleep in my bedroom. Before she crawled into my bed, I placed a cotton pad on her side. Just in case.

I pulled out my phone and decided to check a few emails and respond to some text messages. While clearing a few junk messages, I landed on a thread with an old friend. Regardless of how many times I updated and changed my phone over the course of fifteen years. I was happy for Apple that the messages followed, and I was ever careful not to delete them.

After that painful night in the hospital, I couldn't get myself to respond to any of his attempts to reach out to me. I could barely peel myself out of bed for months. The grief after the loss of my father was all too much to bear. I saw someone briefly to teach me how to cope, but I never really finished that course of treatment. Eventually, life continued, and before I knew it, I had much bigger fish to fry than sitting on a couch combing through my mismanaged loss. Once I was back to myself, I felt it was too late. After so much time had passed, what would I say?

"Mommy, are you looking at forever bae's text messages again?" Peyton lifted her head and grabbed my phone.

"Peyton, go to bed."

When Peyton was younger, she would ask me to read her bedtime stories, and over the years, that turned into her asking me to tell her my own. One night, because I have no filter with my daughter, I shared with her my unfinished story with my friend, Old. She coined the term "forever bae," and that's how we've referred to him since.

I held out my hand, and she gave me back my phone before turning on her back.

"What's the worst that could happen? You've literally left him on read for years. If he doesn't respond, at least you tried. C'mon, Mom. Be brave."

I thought back to the times when my father said I was fearless or called me a dare devil like my mother. Brave I was. But vulnerable? Openly emotionally? Sensitive? Those were all risks I considered to be far more deadly than climbing Mount Kilimanjaro.

"I wouldn't even know what to say. And what if he responded? Then what? I can think of a million things that could go wrong here. Actually, we're not having this conversation." I slunk into bed and laid my head on my pillow, determined to call it a night.

"I know we're new to this religion thing, but at school, they said that Jesus is hope. And while I don't fully know what that means yet, I'm sure it means if your trust is in Jesus, you shouldn't be a punk."

ALL THINGS BEAUTIFUL

The last country we lived in before moving to Atlanta was Spain, and there we met a devout older Christian woman who prayed and fasted often. Her devotion and belief in something unexplainable fascinated me. I asked her questions, and to the best of her ability, because I knew very little conversational Spanish, she read the Bible to me. When Peyton and I picked a school for her to attend, we picked a private Christian school. She wanted to grow more in her relationship with God, and I wanted that for her. I wanted that for me as well but hadn't really gotten around to it yet.

"I think you've got that wrong, and I think Jesus would say you're manipulating me." I sighed. "But I'll text him."

"Really! You promise?"

In the cool blue light of my phone, I could see Peyton smiling from ear to ear. I couldn't lie to her. And would Jesus want me to be a punk?

"I promise."

CHAPTER 2

> Happy belated birthday.

I had just finished spending some time in prayer when my phone chirped. I looked at the screen and immediately dropped it. If I wasn't already kneeling against my bed, I would've fallen to the ground.

Her number wasn't saved anymore. I deleted our messages and call history years ago. But looking at my phone, I immediately knew, and that revelation was excitingly terrifying.

"That can't be.... No. There's no way. No."

I silenced my phone, added another final prayer, and went to bed.

***

"Daddy? Daddy! Good morning."

"Daddy! Wake up, sleepy head!"

The tiny hands of my five-year-olds kept pushing and poking my sides. I squinted and held one eye open. "What time is it?"

"It says it's 5 hours and 3 minutes."

"No, silly; it's 5 and 3 *0* minutes."

"It's 5:30, girls. That means it's still bedtime." I threw the comforter off my body and grabbed a girl in each arm, nestling them in bed with me.

"Daddy, I'm not sleepy anymore. Can we wake up now?" Hope yawned.

Hope rubbed her hand on my beard, and soon Grace joined in.

"Yeah, Daddy. Let's make breakfast," Grace cooed.

I loved these little girls more than anything on the planet, but this was getting old, fast.

"Wake-up time is at 6:30. We can get up today…" I shifted my face to Grace, who was now dancing and clapping. "But tomorrow, you're both going to stay in your own beds until the alarm goes off. Big girls stay in their own beds and wait until the sun rises. Serious face."

Hope and Grace now matched my expression and furrowed their eyebrows together with tight lips.

"I promise, Daddy. I'm a big girl, and I can stay in my own bed," Hope declared, jumping off the bed.

"I'm a big girl, too. Right, Daddy?"

"You're both big girls. Now, let's pray and get started."

I ran my hand down my face and picked Grace off the bed before setting her on the ground. We said a quick morning prayer and were off.

In the past five years, we've gotten our morning routine down to a science. And that science was basically running around like chickens, getting them to make their beds, remembering to make mine, getting them dressed and changed into their school uniforms, making breakfast, cleaning up after breakfast, getting myself ready for work, packing their lunches, and combing their hair. We turned every day into a race, challenge, or some sort of game to get it all done without ruining the house. Depending on the day, they would either giggle or fight the entire time, but we made it out of the house on time and alive, which is the part that mattered most.

"Daddy, I want three ponytails, not two." Grace pouted, and she held up three tiny fingers.

"I don't think that's a thing, Gracey. I've never seen three ponytails."

"Yes, huh, it is, Daddy," Hope chimed in to defend her sister.

I looked at them, and they were both now pouting, pulling on every single last heart string.

"Okay. I'll look up three ponytails on Pinterest today. And maybe we can ask Titi Nicky. But for right now, I only have two ponytails in me. I'm only a man; Daddy's sorry."

"It's okay, Daddy. Two ponytails is still pretty." Grace wrapped her arm around my neck and kissed my cheek.

"Yeah, Daddy. You'll get better. Be strong, remember?" Hope held up and flexed both of her arms.

I laughed. "Yeah, yeah. That's right, Hopey."

***

Chestmire Christian Academy was a private K-12 institution. The girls had to be in school no later than 9:30 a.m. but could get there as early as 6:30 a.m. for extra tuition, of course.

I dropped them off at eight every morning so I could have a minute to myself before the middle school classes started at 9:45 a.m. The students at Chestmire were some of the best and brightest, and if they didn't fall into that category that meant their parents were loaded.

Teaching here was a breath of fresh air, compared to the public schools in the inner cities I used to work at. I missed my old students and still kept in contact with a few of them to ensure they were maintaining their grades. One kid in particular even invited me to his graduation because he was sure he would graduate now and attributed that success to me not giving up on him. I thought about each of them and prayed for them regularly. I felt a strong pull to teach here, though, and I learned to listen to that gentle voice a long time ago. It always led me to exactly where I needed to be.

The extra income was an added bonus, not to mention being much closer to the girls. It was also refreshing to have students whom I didn't need to earn their respect and who were actually interested in the assigned readings. Still, in every class, there was always at least one student who stood out among the many.

"Mr. Timothy. So, I went over the reading list with my mom this morning, and she pointed out that if the school is going to ban certain non-fiction books because of violence, then I shouldn't be allowed to read this." Peyton, one of my promising, well-read, and well-spoken students, slid Homer's *The Odyssey* on my desk. "She says that many of the books on the banned/parental discretion advised list were monumental to the strife and successes of black and indigenous peoples in this country. And that books like *The Odyssey* are just as graphic, horrific, and broadcast white Eurocentric views of sexism that are outdated and repugnant."

I picked up the book. "She said all that, did she?"

There was always one parent every year, without fail.

"She did. Verbatim." She then lowered her voice into a whisper, "But between you and me, she's a handful. And besides, we read this together a few years ago. I forgot to mention this one yesterday."

I chuckled in amusement. "Believe me, I get it. *The Odyssey* is great; a classic. But not my favorite. We'll find something to replace it with."

She smiled and took victorious strides back to her seat. Her honey-infused eyes and brown hair looked oddly familiar.

In the story, Penelope waits for her husband Odysseus for twenty years while he wages war and travels a long-winded journey back home. I don't know if that's the epitome of love in all its glory or just tragic. Have I been waiting for fifteen years? I thought back to the text message and remembered a girl who made me feel tingles and butterflies from miles, space, and years away. A girl who I'd willingly walk over hot coals to be next to her, but that was years ago. I pulled myself out of those thoughts and continued with class.

***

"Bro, get your head in the game. You mean to tell me you still haven't texted her back? You're tripping."

"Text back and say what exactly?" I held up my phone and fixed it on my desk so I could talk and eat without holding it.

"How about you tell her that you moved to Atlanta nine years ago in hopes that you'd run into her?"

"I didn't move here for her."

"Yeah, okay. And why did you, then?" He waited briefly, then smugly responded, "No answer? Exactly."

I looked at my brother Eden as he also ate his lunch. While we didn't quite see eye to eye for most of our growing up, things really did turn around for him after his last hospitalization fifteen years ago. He said he had a real encounter with God in a dream and that he was going to change his life. He spent the next year at rehab and soon after joined a seminary school. He now travels alongside his wife, Daisha, sharing the gospel and ministering to teens and youths also struggling with drugs and alcohol.

It took a while for our relationship to be mended, but he didn't stop trying. Soon enough, I forgave him—for hurting me, bullying me, and neglecting me when all I wanted from him was friendship. Even in the timing of things, God is faithful because if it wasn't for him, I'm not sure how I would've gotten over my then-girlfriend not answering any of my calls.

We made it a thing to always eat lunch together Monday through Friday if the time zone he was in allowed.

After graduating, I felt another one of those urges, leading me to move to Atlanta. At the time, I hoped that it would be to find and reconnect with her again. Although I didn't, what I did end up finding was still valuable and good in its own way.

Daisha walked up behind Eden and kissed his cheek before wrapping her arms around his neck.

"Hey there, Z!" Daisha smiled at the screen.

"Hey, Daisha! How are you?"

We all spoke for a few more minutes before I needed to end the call. I spent my free period eating lunch and then getting the girls from school to bring them to Nicole at the community center for her REACH program.

***

"And, Daddy, Simon said Hope is bigger than me, too. Is she bigger than me?" Grace asked, frowning. Her ponytails completely disheveled from the school day.

"That's because I am bigger than you, Gracey," Hope proclaimed loudly as I fastened her in her booster seat. Her hair was also equally disheveled.

"Technically…" I sat in the front seat and fastened my own seat belt. "You're both the same size. But Hope is three minutes older than you, Grace. It's not a lot, but she's still the biggest in that way."

Hope cheered, and Grace's frown deepened.

"Grace did weigh more, though, for that first day, so she's a little bigger, too. See, you're both bigger, just in different ways."

Grace started to smile and tap at her iPad, satisfied with my answer.

I adjusted the rear-view mirror to be able to see them both clearly with the backseat mirror. Hope was looking at me and smiled mischievously.

"Daddy," she cooed.

Oh boy. "Yes, princess?"

"Do you have to be married for us to get a new mommy? Or can we just pick a new mommy?"

"I would have to get married. But you do have a mommy, remember?"

They did this often. Ask questions and make demands. Usually, I was patient enough to handle them all until it came to my late wife, Melissa. I tried to see the situation from their fresh perspectives. They didn't understand how a woman in a picture was a mother to them. Not when they saw mothers dropping off their classmates and kissing boo-boos. I couldn't understand how they didn't look at those same pictures and see someone timeless. Classic. Irreplaceable.

I immediately felt a quick wash of guilt. Melissa was—no—is irreplaceable. In a way that apparently only I could understand.... New, however, is begrudgingly unforgettable. In a way I don't understand.

"We know, Daddy. We know that. But we need a real mommy who can do three ponytails," Grace testified, holding up three fingers again.

Hope nodded her head vigorously in agreement.

"I found a picture today, and I can give you three ponytails tomorrow."

"Okay. Fine." Grace looked over to her sister, who whispered something to her.

Hope perked up. "Daddy, Ms. Z is really pretty. She's an artist, and she showed us how to paint, and she had on really cool orange sneakers, and she is so beautiful, like a princess."

Grace now nodded her head. "You can come inside to meet her, Daddy. She's really, really nice and she gave us snacks. And she talked about all the pretty colors because she's so smart. Like you, Daddy."

Are my five-year-olds really trying to set me up? "I can't go inside. You guys know that. I have to get back before 3 p.m. to finish my classes."

I pulled up to the community center and texted Nicole. Within a few minutes, she was outside helping me to unbuckle the girls.

"Hey, Z! Heyyy, Hopey and Gracey. We have to move really fast today because Ms. Z has a special surprise just for you."

Both girls hopped and cheered at the sound of that news. I decided to get out of the car and have a quick talk with Nicole.

"Hey, girls, let me talk to your Titi. Go wait for her by the door." I kissed both of them, and they raced to the door. Hope made it first, and then they started to squabble.

"What's up? Is everything good?" Nicole asked, holding her hand above her head to shield her eyes from the sun.

"Yeah, all good. It has been non-stop Ms. Z talk since last night. You know how the girls can get. I just don't want them getting too attached, and today they're going on and on about a new mommy, and I just wanted to make sure they aren't getting the wrong idea."

"No way," Nicole remarked, giggling. "She's my next-door neighbor and just moved here a few weeks ago. She's cool people, I swear."

I shrugged, unsure if that answer was enough but too pressed for time to sort through my thoughts. Not to mention, I didn't need to throw in the idea of a third woman to the ball toss happening in my head.

Nicole nudged my shoulder and shrugged. "Be cool. They're safe here with me, and I trust her. And with all that mommy stuff, I don't know. Maybe they have a sense about her, too."

ALL THINGS BEAUTIFUL

***

After the workday, I made my way over to Nicole's. She had taken the girls with her since I was running late from a staff meeting.

I knocked on her front door to announce my arrival before letting myself in.

"Daddy!" both girls sang in unison and held up their arms.

I grabbed hold of them both and swung them around before placing them on the couch.

"It smells good in here; what are you cooking up?" I asked Nicole, who was moving back and forth from the pantry to the island in a daze.

"It's for my neighbor, Z. She decided to join the REACH team and I promised I would make her dinner and banana pudding for helping me out. She's an amazing artist, and I'm happy to have her. She and her daughter are going to come over to celebrate." Nicole faced me with a suspicious grin. "You should stay and meet her. I was able to talk to Hope and Grace, and they both are smitten with her. I know for a fact she's single, and you never know."

I ran my hand down my face and sighed. "Not you, too. I'm more than capable of finding myself a wife…and I don't even know if I'm interested in dating anyone right now. Besides, the girls already have a mother."

I looked down at my empty ring finger. The lighter band of skin had long since faded over the years. The patch of skin had clearly moved on, the verdict was still out on my heart.

Nicole put down whatever concoction she was holding and grabbed my hand. "Hey. I know you loved my sister, but it is okay to move on. The girls had a mother they were far too young to even remember. They need a mom now. They need a mom for all the things that you won't be able to handle."

"That's what you're here for. To have all the girl conversations about periods and hair and whatever else they'll need to talk about."

"Take it from someone who still calls her mom regularly; it's not the same thing. Just think it over, Z. And maybe it won't be my neighbor, who knows. Just be open to the idea because you don't just need someone for them but for you too."

Some one.

"Oh wow, I just realized you're Z, and she's Z. How funny is that." Nicole's smile widened. "Sounds like a match made in heaven to me…even if you won't stick around long enough to meet her."

I shook my head. Nicole was a hopeless, whatever the cost, love never fails, die-hard romantic. She's never tried to set me up before but started to make subtle hints three years ago that I should start dating.

"It doesn't matter. I can't stay anyway."

She frowned but relented and walked us to the door.

After buckling the girls into the car, I started to back out of the driveway when a cherry red Lexus pulled in. I felt almost tempted to wait it out and see who got out of the car but instead decided to respond to a text that had been burning a hole in my pocket all day.

> Happy belated birthday.
> How have you been, New?

CHAPTER 3

"Peyton!" I yelled out my open car window.

Peyton looked at me and waved before hugging everyone in the circle that sat around her. She walked swiftly towards the car.

"Hey, Mom! How was your day?" Peyton kissed me on the cheek before buckling up.

"It was really good. I finished up that 'lady in the tree' sculpture. How was yours, and who are all these kids? More new friends?"

In the past two weeks of school, Peyton had made more friends than I could keep up with. I was so happy for her. She stayed true to her spunk and found people who liked her for it. Her closest friends were Jasmine and Paige, who had been over to our house for dinner on two occasions. Peyton said everyone referred to me as the cool mom.

I was open with all of them, mainly because I wanted to sniff out if anyone had bad intentions. Jasmine and Paige were your typical run-of-the-mill eleven-year-olds, so for now, they were both okay in my book.

"Since it's early release, today we decided to have

ALL THINGS BEAUTIFUL

group therapy. Marcus and Aaliyah had a huge fight because Marcus decided to sit next to Lexi at lunch. Which basically erupted the entire homeostasis of the school because Aaliyah and Lexi are sworn mortal enemies. But I was able to help all parties find a way to bury the hatchet. Marcus apologized to Aaliyah, and Aaliyah apologized to Lexi. At the root of everything, Lexi was jealous of Aaliyah for getting a boyfriend before her. We're going to continue our session Monday."

I rolled my eyes. "Sounds like a Shakespearian play. Sworn mortal enemies? And boyfriends? Who has a boyfriend in sixth grade?"

Peyton let out a heavy breath. "Mom, almost everyone has a boyfriend in sixth grade. We're not in elementary school anymore. We're growing up; our bodies are changing, not to mention the hormones in our bloodstream. It's a lot to deal with."

"I know, I know. And trust me, I remember." I pulled into the community center and parked my car, facing Peyton and folding my leg in the cushioned seat. "What about you? Any boys you're interested in?"

"Get a grip, Mommy. None of these guys have a single clue yet. I won't be dating until I have established myself as a famous psychotherapist and author. I have too much to do to be getting gaga over the male specimen."

I silently thanked God and kissed her cheek. She might

not always feel that way, but it was more than enough solace for now.

"You're way too smart for your own good, you know that?"

"I know. What about you and your boyfriend?" Peyton put her face on her layered hands and made kissing faces at me.

"I don't have a boyfriend."

"You don't have a boyfriend *yet*. It's all about perspective, Mom. Let me see your phone. What did you guys talk about today?"

I handed her my phone, and I laughed as she analyzed our texts. After all this time, one text message propelled me back to meeting him in Aspen, falling for him in Myrtle Beach, kissing him in Charleston, and leaving him in the hospital that same day.

"Mom, you need to lay it on him because this is going nowhere fast."

"I wouldn't say that…" I chewed my lip. "It's just different. We're older now. And this is just old friends catching up. Nothing serious."

"Puh-lease. You've caught up on the weather sixty-four times here. You didn't even mention me, so basically, you're both talking about a lot of nothing."

ALL THINGS BEAUTIFUL

She was right. While all the feelings I had for him resurfaced, so much time and life had happened since I last saw him. I had no idea how to connect with him anymore; he could be somewhere married for all I know.

"What if he's married? Or in a serious relationship? Maybe that's why nothing has picked up."

"I don't think so because even though you're both extremely boring, he responds quickly to every one of your texts. Aaliyah can't even get Marcus to do that. He's feeling you, Mom. He just doesn't know if you're feeling him, so he's playing it safe. I bet if you up the ante, he would respond well."

Nicole's car pulled up next to us in the lot. After waving, she got out of her car to pull out various props for the theatre. Peyton and I hopped out to give her a hand.

"Hey, girlfriends!" Nicole sang in her usual cheerleader tone. "Thanks so much for coming to help us on your early release day."

"No prob. I'm looking forward to meeting the little kiddos. Especially since my mom isn't giving me a sibling anytime soon with the way her dating life is going." Peyton snickered amusingly.

I kicked the back of her leg gently with my knee.

"You're dating? I didn't know that! You have to tell me everything."

Nicole was slender and petite. All of her muscles were toned undoubtedly attributed to her previous dance career. She was fair-skinned, with full lips and black wavy hair that curled at the ends and at the nape of her neck. I'd learned that Nicole was mixed, but she always emphasized that her mother was black and said that made all the difference. She used to dance ballet with a company in New York, but after experiencing her second stress fracture, she decided to spend some time with her family.

She explained that the timing of everything was purposeful because her sister passed, leaving her brother-in-law with two newborns. I didn't pry much on that topic because I knew firsthand how messy it could get unpacking grief.

Nicole, in all her moxie, quickly became the friend I needed years ago but was happy to have now. She was slowly uncovering all the layers that took a lifetime to build, effortlessly.

"I didn't tell you because there isn't anything to tell. He's an old friend—"

"Not just a friend," Peyton interrupted. "He's her forever bae."

While setting up and ensuring we were ready for drop off, Peyton caught Nicole up on all the details of my "forever bae."

"I agree with Peyton here. I was secretly hoping to be able to set you up with my brother, but this guy sounds way more charming. Not that my brother isn't; I'm sure you both would hit it off. But since you and this guy have so much history, maybe you should throw out a line and see if he bites."

"Thank you! See, Mom? Nicole gets it."

Peyton and Nicole high-fived and continued to talk about what I should text back.

Watching them carry out a conversation seamlessly made the corners of my mouth turn up. I expected this but didn't realize how much I wanted it. For her entire life and so much of mine, it has been just us. While our relationship meant the world to me, I didn't want to be the only one in her world. That's just too fragile, too fleeting, too fatal.

I swallowed my arising feelings of hurt and willed myself not to go back there. I'm here, in this moment, and I'm okay.

"Okay, okay," I chimed in. "I'll send him a text now."

> "Hey, what city do you live in?"

Old, "I've actually been wanting to ask you. But I wasn't sure if that was another one of your don't tell rules."

> Old, "I'm in Atlanta.
> What about yourself?"

"Oh my gosh! He says he lives in Atlanta, guys. Is this real life, or is this a joke?" I started pacing the gymnasium with my eyes glued to the screen.

Peyton and Nicole started cheering in the background while I responded.

> "Oh wow. I'm actually in Atlanta, too."

> Old, "What would you say to meeting up? Maybe coffee or lunch?"

I looked up from my screen to a still-roaring Peyton and Nicole. "He asked me if I wanted to have coffee or lunch. How should I respond?"

Peyton and Nicole began deliberating the pros and cons of doing a morning meet up versus an afternoon one.

> Old, "Let's actually do dinner.
> That is if that's okay with you."

"No, you guys! He said, 'Let's do dinner instead.'" I turned my phone so that Peyton could read the text and then showed it to Nicole.

"Okay, girl. This isn't just a casual meet-up anymore; this is officially a date." Nicole did a little dance.

"Okay. Respond, Mom! You've got him right where you want him." Peyton stood on her tiptoes and tried to watch as I typed.

> "Thursday night?"

> Old, "I can't. I have an open house that night. How about Friday?"

"I think he also has kids because he said he has to attend an open house on Thursday. Oh shoot, that's right! Your open house is Thursday, too." I looked over at Peyton who was so overcome with excitement she was nearing bursting into literal flames.

"Friday, Mom! Do Friday!"

"I can't do Friday. That's our movie night, Peyton."

"I'll stay home alone. I'm mature enough. Or I can stay the night at Nicole's. Right, Nicole?"

I gave Peyton the "don't impose on other adults the way you do me and embarrass me" look. She nodded her head in acknowledgment.

"That's fine with me," Nicole added while answering a text message of her own.

"I'll think about it and respond later."

"But Mom…this is a once in a lifetime."

I interrupted her, "I'll respond later."

I wasn't sure if I was nervous about actually seeing him in person or slightly offended by Peyton wanting to share our ritual Friday night movie night with Nicole. Perhaps it was a mix of both. Either way, I will respond later. *Maybe*.

"That's my brother. I'm going to step out and get the girls. I'll be right back." Nicole walked to the front door and was greeted by a man.

I turned away and looked at Peyton, who was now scrolling on her phone with her headphones in her ears. Didn't the possibility of not spending a Friday night together bother her?

***

"This was actually fun, Mom. And it was so cool watching you do your thing. You're my inspiration, you know that."

"Awww. You're sweet for saying that, dude."

"And you were right; Hope and Grace were the most adorable little girls on the planet." Peyton put her legs up on the dashboard and reclined her seat. "How cool would it be if I had *two* sisters…"

"Do you need a puppy or something? You've been banging out this sibling idea a little hard recently."

"I'm not a puppy person or a cat person, for that matter. I'm a people person. So get to it." Peyton snapped her fingers, making us both laugh, and she leaned her head into my shoulder.

"It's not that simple, baby. I wish it was, but it isn't."

"Yeah, I know…" Peyton shifted her position and dropped her legs.

I often wondered if Peyton was lonely. As much as my father meant to me, he couldn't be everything and everyone I needed. There were times I felt lonely, too. I didn't have siblings and cousins growing up. I didn't want to deny her that family experience; it just wasn't something I could produce or work up myself.

I used car play to FaceTime her dad, Eddie.

"Hey XYZ, can I call you back?" Peyton turned her face from the window and looked at him on the screen. "PeyPey! Hey, Daddy's girl!"

"Hello, Father. How are you?" Peyton picked up my phone from the hands-free device.

"Ooosh. Cold shoulder," Eddie said with a confused

face. "What did I do now?"

Eddie and I met during my senior year of college. At that point in my life, I was overwhelmed with grief and sinking in midterms. It was two years to the date of my father's passing. I should have taken the summer semester off, but at that time, I couldn't stand to sit alone with my thoughts.

I decided to go to a party late one night and met him. He wasn't a student at Stanford but went to USC to study video game design and programming. He was interesting and made me laugh, and all I wanted in that season of my life was someone to help me bury all of my sadness.

We spent a few years in an on-again-off-again relationship up until I found out I was pregnant. We tried to make things become something permanent and long-term for a hot three seconds before realizing we were never going to work.

We had joint custody for a few years, even though that really meant he would pop by to see her one or two Saturdays a month. When a developer reached out to him about producing a game he had been working on, he had to do a lot of traveling back and forth to Los Angeles. I took that opportunity to become a nomad with my then five-year-old. We tried to FaceTime one another once a week, but that was a difficult thing to maintain, mainly due to his scheduling conflicts.

ALL THINGS BEAUTIFUL

While Eddie and Peyton were, what some might say, a bit estranged, I still hoped he could fill in in ways that I know only a father could. Because now, it was evident that in this season, we both needed more people.

CHAPTER 4

"I can take that on. I didn't play in college or anything, but I did play varsity in both junior and senior high."

"Why, Mr. Timothy, you are a man of many, many talents, I see." Caitlyn licked her lips so forcefully that I could hear them smack across the teacher's lounge.

Chestmire was known for having several events and fundraisers each season; this meeting was to plan the Harvest Fest that would be taking place the first week in October. With as much as I paid for tuition for my kids to go to kindergarten and recite ABCs all day, I highly doubted they were in need of a fundraiser. Nonetheless, I wanted to participate and thought playing basketball with some of the other teachers and parents here would be fun.

I smiled politely and looked down at my phone. Still no response from New.

I'm not sure if asking her out to dinner was too forward or if that made her uncomfortable. I'm not sure what the issue could have been, quite honestly. I was relieved to be talking to her about anything else other than the temperatures finally dropping into the mid-sixties.

When she asked me what city I was in, I thought that

was a clear sign that I could make a move. But then again, maybe I was just reading into things. I had been glued to my phone in the weeks since she sent that first text. Even though we were talking about a whole lot of nothing, I was still talking to *her*.

I shook my head and put my phone back in my pocket. I needed to pull myself together and focus on my girls. Perhaps it was a good thing that we didn't reconnect. I've wondered all these years about her, and now I know. She's alive. She's okay. Opening myself back up to her would mean creating space, and if she was still as golden and magnetic as I remember, I would need more than just a coat closet, bottom drawer kind of space. I patted down my pants and straightened my tie before tossing away my half-empty cup of coffee. I took focused strides towards my classroom to prepare for my next class.

"Mr. Timothy, can I actually speak with you for a moment? This will just be a minute." Caitlyn placed a hand on my arm as I opened my door.

I must've subconsciously looked at her hand because she removed it and let out an awkward laugh.

"How can I help you, Mrs. Coleman?" I decided against closing the classroom door completely and left it open a crack.

"Well, it's just that. It's Ms. Coleman. Not Mrs.," she corrected before sitting in a student seat and crossing her legs up high enough to make her skirt rise.

"Okay, *Ms.* Coleman. Do you need me to assist you with something else for the festival?"

I could tell by her seductive mannerism and flirtatious tone that she wasn't here for help or assistance, at least not in a way that involved any students or the school. What she wanted was something I had no plans of giving to her.

"I actually wanted to know if you'd be interested in heading out with me for drinks after the festival or maybe a movie. It's your choice, really." Caitlyn licked her lips again and eyed me from head to toe hungrily.

"Oh. I'm sorry, but I'll be with my children after the festival. They've made it clear they wanted to try making it out of the corn maze and take pictures in the pumpkin patch. I'm sure you and the other teachers and staff will have a great time, though."

Caitlyn gave me a glowering look. She was undoubtedly a beautiful woman and probably used to getting her way with men. This was her second time shooting her shot and her second time being rejected. I didn't have a type or anything, but for whatever reason, I knew she wasn't it.

"Okay, well. I guess I'll be seeing you." She got up and sashayed her way out of my classroom, making sure to swing her hips with each stride.

Caitlyn's overexerted walk, made me think of someone

much more effortless.

I reached for my phone and checked my text messages again. Still nothing.

"Pull it together, man," I said to myself out loud.

My phone rang, and for a brief second, I hoped it would be her.

I answered, "Hey man, what's up?"

"Not much. Did you skip lunch today or something?" Eden asked, not looking at the phone.

"Naw. I ate lunch in the lounge today. There was a meeting."

"Oh, okay. Cool, cool." Eden was still looking away from the screen.

"Is everything good with you, man?" I inquired since he was acting strange.

"Yeah, yeah. All is good. Daisha hasn't been feeling too well, so I'm just keeping an eye out for her."

Eden met Daisha while in seminary school. Her testimony was similar to his, except her addiction wasn't to drugs or alcohol; it was to people's opinions. Equally debilitating if you ask me. They clicked immediately and were married within three months of meeting. To know Eden was to know he would do anything for her, so I'm sure he was going through it not being able to help her feel better.

"You want to say a quick prayer?" I asked, causing his demeanor to change, and he faced me.

"Yeah, let's do that."

I bowed my head, closed my eyes, and took a minute to rest in the presence of God before speaking. "Precious Lord, I thank You because I know from experience that You are good and Your grace is unending. At this moment, I ask that You comfort and heal Your daughter. You created her, and You know all of her innermost parts. I ask that whatever this is be turned around for her good. I also ask that You would be a comfort to Your son in this moment and that all of his worries and anxieties be cast on You, and in their place, You'd give him perfect peace. Thank You, Father. In Jesus' name, amen." I opened my eyes and found Eden still had his eyes closed. I gave him the space to hear and be moved by the Spirit.

"I just feel heavy right now in my spirit that God is asking me to tell you to stay encouraged and that He has heard you." Eden opened his eyes and laughed. "Any idea what that could be about?"

"No clue whatsoever, but I receive it anyway." I chortled.

We talked for a few minutes more and ended the call.

ALL THINGS BEAUTIFUL

One more time, I checked my phone. Still, no response. I decided that maybe I was too forward and charged it. I was glad to know that she was okay, and I hoped that wherever she was, she was also happy.

***

Tonight, I had orientation for two out of the six classes I taught. Last week, the school held an open house for grades nine through twelve, and today, we were hosting the parents of children in grades six through eight. Most educators I knew despised middle schoolers because they were caught someplace in between still being very much children and also trying to enter the early stages of young adulthood. Not to mention, twenty kids in a classroom all experiencing puberty made for some interesting stories.

I reveled in being able to educate them, though. While high school was smoother, especially in junior year, where kids were focused on testing and college applications, middle school had its own personal flare. The kids were still impressionable and made way for multiple opportunities to course-correct the ones who needed an extra push and some guidance in the right direction.

My eighth-grade class went by smoothly since most of the parents and students have been here for three years minimum. I knew sixth grade was going to be full of parents with questions about the curriculum and grading criteria, as I already had a line outside and wrapped around the hallway.

I opened the door and jammed a door-stopper to keep it open. "Welcome, welcome, everyone. If you can fit in a seat, you're welcome to do so, and if you cannot much like myself, well, just pick a spot on the wall."

A few parents laughed as they walked in and flooded the room.

I queued up the PowerPoint presentation I prepared for the evening and began scanning the room to greet each parent with my eyes. Or whatever the admin is pushing these days. "Okay, ladies and gentlemen, it is my pleasure to meet you all, the lucky parents of the future. I am Mr. Timothy, and I…" While scanning the room, my eyes landed on the purest honey-colored set of eyes I think I'd ever seen.

She didn't need to announce herself, I knew. And instantly, in front of everyone in the room, I became a twelve-year-old boy all over again. She wore her hair curly still, like I remembered, only now the dark colors of brown intertwined with lightened strands of blonde. She wore a black *Avengers* tee shirt and paired it with black biker shorts that exposed her toned brown legs. She wore a green blazer and black heels.

I remember her sharing during one conversation that heels were torture weapons created in favor of the patriarchy. I let out a small laugh at that memory. I wonder what else about her has changed.

At the sound of my laugh, her eyes lifted and found mine. And in front of everyone, I watched her become a twelve-year-old girl. After all these years, again, we reconnected. This time, not on vacation or on a short trip where we were trying to race an ever-speeding clock, not over coffee or dinner as I had proposed, but in a place where we both, hopefully, had time.

And space.

I gave the presentation as thoroughly as I rehearsed, but my focus was on her.

***

After the presentation and several rounds of questioning, parents started to leave my classroom for their children's next class. A few parents came up to greet me personally, and while I did my best to give them the attention they needed, my eyes were fixed on her.

It seemed as if she and Peyton were going back and forth about something, and when she got up to head towards the door, Peyton made some sort of signal that made her decide to change her mind and head my way.

She's headed straight towards me.

She cleared her throat and smiled. "Hi."

One word in, and I was already hers.

"Hiii, Mr. Timothy. This is my mom. Mom, obviously, this is Mr. Timothy." Peyton introduced us formally before giving her mom a conniving grin.

I wondered if she knew about our history.

"Hi. Nice to meet you, Ms...." I extended my hand.

"Ms. Smith."

She extended her hand back towards me and shook it, lighting a fire that you couldn't see or smell but one that could most certainly be felt. She looked down at our hands briefly before letting it go. She sat on one of the students' desks and looked around. I did the same and waited until the last parent was out of the classroom.

"So, I guess I should explain." She looked down at her heels and wiggled her feet inside of her shoes.

"Okay." I folded my arms across my chest, unsure if she was explaining why she didn't text me back yesterday or why she stopped texting me back years ago. Unsure if I was ready to hear either of those truths.

She lifted her face and just stared at me, searching my eyes. Not saying anything, but in some way saying everything.

"Eh-hum." Peyton cleared her throat. "I'm really sorry to break up this reunion; I can only imagine all the things that need to be said. But yet, and still, I have one more class to go to, and it's Algebra 1, and Mom, I really need you to scare Mrs. Walker straight."

I laughed. "I've heard Mrs. Walker can be tough. But I think she'll grow on you," I answered, still looking at her as she got up from the desk.

"I know I didn't respond, but...I would lov—like to have dinner with you tomorrow. If the offer is still available."

"It is." I moved closer to her before I could remember that her daughter, my student, was still watching this entire interaction.

I took a step back but smiled, glad that of all the things that might've changed, she still had the same sweet smell of vanilla and argan oil.

She extended her hand again and smiled. "My name is Zipporah."

The smile on my face widened, and like a rushing wind, all the moments and near misses that led us both up to this moment ran through my mind. I extended my hand and held on to hers for the last time tonight.

"My name is Zaire."

CHAPTER 5

"Mom! You can't wear jeans to a dinner date. Especially not on a first date!" Peyton bossed, running around in my closet, looking through all the imaginary dresses I didn't have. "Ugh. Have I taught you nothing?"

"Sweet P, this isn't a first date. This is just dinner between friends." I had said that multiple times today, trying my darndest to convince her and myself.

Peyton stopped dead in her tracks and looked at me. "Be so for real, Mom. This is a date." She then went back to ransacking my closet.

In all honesty, I didn't want Peyton's hopes to be up prematurely. After last night, she had spoken non-stop about Mr. Timothy, my "forever bae," and how fate had brought us together. I wasn't sure about that, but I knew I also didn't want to get my hopes up. Still, parts of me couldn't help but wonder, hope, and imagine.

Zaire.

He looked so different I almost would've missed him, but his eyes and that laugh gave it all away. That and the way he looked at me, like no one but him has ever done before. He had cut his locs and sported a shorter haircut with faded sides. His eyebrows were dark and smoldering, as were his full lips and his smile. His face was handsome and chiseled better than anything I could work up with clay. His beard was clean-cut and shaved low to his face. His freckles had faded only a bit and seemed to be more dispersed throughout his face. His body was toned and muscular, and even though he was wearing a shirt and tie, you could easily see the thickness of his arms. The man was fine.

"Mommy, you have to wear this!" Peyton came out of my closet with a black midi-length dress that had a split on the side and a sweetheart neckline.

"Peyton! That's a bit much for a first date, I think."

She looked at me and twisted her face into a scowl. "Mom. Trust me. This is the dress you want to wear tonight."

I complied and started getting ready for the evening. Peyton also took it upon herself to flat iron my hair and shape it into a long angled bob and did a light touch of makeup.

I took a final glance in the mirror and felt deeply impressed with how well Peyton put everything together.

"Wow, Sweet P. You're amazing. You know that, right?"

"I know. We both are." Peyton stepped on my vanity chair and sat on the edge of the bathroom sink. "I told you,

you're *that* girl."

I shook my head and laughed. I turned around to pack all my things in the world's tiniest purse, but the one she said "set the dress off."

"Are your things all packed for Nicole's tonight?"

"Yup. I just need to figure out what *I'm* going to be wearing. I'm going to pick something based on the theme of the movie or based on how I feel. We'll see." Peyton shrugged.

With my purse now packed, I walked over to the kitchen table, and she followed behind me.

"Mom, can I ask you a question?"

I looked at Peyton's face as she chewed on her lip.

"What's up, Sweet P? Talk to me."

Before she could answer, my phone rang and announced I was getting an incoming call from Old.

Peyton and I both looked at my phone lying on the kitchen table.

"Oh, no. Do you think he's canceling?"

"No. I don't think so, but hurry up and answer, Mom," she urged.

"Hey…hey. Hi, hello." Not only did this man have the

ability to make me nervous, but now he had me babbling like a two-year-old.

"Hey...New?" He sounded like he asked, sounding unsure of how he should refer to me. I guess I had similar questions.

"Yeah. Hey. Is everything still good? Are we still on for tonight or..."

"No. No. We're most certainly still on. I just had my babysitter cancel on me last minute, and I need to now bring my daughters to my parent's home. They live on the opposite side of town, and I don't want us to miss our reservation. Is it okay if I send a car to your home to pick you up?"

"Ohhh. Oh, okay. But I don't mind driving." As the words left my mouth, Peyton shook her head no.

"No. I still want to be able to bring you home after tonight. I do apologize for this last-minute change."

"It's okay. I get it. Sure, you can send a car. Do you need me to text you my address again?"

"Naw, I saved it. I'll let you know when the car is outside."

We exchanged goodbyes and hung up.

***

Together, Peyton and I walked over to Nicole's. She decided to give me pointers on how to behave tonight because she said I obviously had no clue. My eleven-year-old, who was currently eating a popsicle in her unicorn onesie and princess slippers, was giving me dating advice.

"And finally, be observant of everything he does and says. Like does he open your doors, how he talks to the wait staff, and how he treats you and makes you feel."

"That's good advice, Sweet P." I knocked on Nicole's front door.

"I still want to know all the details, but leave out anything yuck since he's my teacher." Peyton scrunched her face.

I laughed. "There won't be anything yucky to report." I stuck my tongue out at her, and she did the same.

Nicole opened the door, "Heyyy! Ooooh…. You're smoking hot, Mamas." Nicole twirled me around and continued to hype up my ensemble. "And what about you! Unicorns, huh? Have you decided what movie we'll be watching?"

We walked into her home, and both sat on her couch.

"I was thinking we should watch *My Little Pony*. I know that sounds childish, but this girl on YouTube gave it a five-star review."

"Oh no." Nicole grabbed her phone. "I wouldn't have canceled on my brother if I knew we were watching something age-appropriate. Let me give him a call." She stepped inside of her kitchen.

"Are you nervous?" Peyton asked.

"Honestly…" I faced her. "Yes and no. More than anything, I am excited to see him and really get to talk to him."

She leaned against me and wrapped an arm around me.

I wrapped my free arm around her and squeezed, "Didn't you say you had something to ask me earlier?"

"Are you going to miss me tonight?"

I kissed the top of her head. "I thought you were okay with me going, Sweet P?"

"I am. I am." Peyton sighed. "If it didn't happen tonight, it would've never happened. But still…Friday's typically our thing."

"Friday still is our thing," I assured her. "And, of course, I'm going to miss you. I miss you already."

"Mom…" She hesitated, which is something she rarely did. "Even if you fall in love with him, which you should. We're still a team, right?"

"We will always be a team, my sassy, smart-mouthed,

brilliant child."

Nicole came out and announced, "His parents are going to drop them off so we can all watch the movie together."

Peyton exclaimed, "That'll be fun. I actually really like Hope and Grace. Maybe we can make cupcakes or something together?"

"That does sound like fun." I cheered, checking my phone. "Okay, this is it. He said the car's outside."

"He sent you a car? How fancy!" Nicole spoke in a fake accent making us laugh.

I hugged and kissed Peyton goodbye.

As I got up and straightened out my dress, Nicole surprisingly pulled me into an embrace. "Have fun tonight. Be open to something new. Call us if anything, especially if he isn't kind."

"He will be. But yeah, if he isn't, call us right away!" Peyton agreed.

They walked me to the door and watched as I got inside the Uber Black parked in front of my house.

***

The Uber parked in front of a restaurant named "La Bonita." The driver got out and escorted me to the door.

ALL THINGS BEAUTIFUL

I walked into a dimly lit room with small, caged fire pits throughout. When I told the hostess the reservation was under Timothy, she led me out back and to the roof. In the center was a large fire pit, a small herb and flower garden off to the side, and near the skyline was the table where he sat.

He got up and walked towards where I stood as the hostess left. His smile grew the closer he came. He extended and opened his hand for mine. I placed it in his and asked myself if this fire that lit every time we touched would faint with time.

"Your beauty is breathtaking."

I smiled in return as he led me towards our table.

"Thank you. You look splendidly handsome yourself."

That he did. He wore a black long-sleeve button-up shirt that emphasized his strong arms and chest, gray slacks, and black loafers.

He pulled out my chair and waited for me to be fully seated before sitting in his own chair.

"When—"

"So how—"

We shared a laugh, and he motioned for me to go first.

"When did you move to Atlanta?"

"A little over nine years ago now. About two years after college." He took a sip of his water and then raised his eyebrow. "Have you always been here?"

"No. I stayed in California for a few years after school and then did a lot of traveling for a few years after that. We only just moved back a few weeks before the school year started."

Our waiter came over and asked if we had any interest in the wine selections after introducing himself. He asked me to pick, so I decided to go with a Merlot.

"You were saying that you traveled. Where are some of the places you lived?"

"Oh wow. We lived in Ghana for two years, which Peyton still swears was her favorite place, although I doubt she remembers most of it. We also lived in London, Canada, Ireland, Haiti, and Spain. Spain was my personal favorite, so I'm actually really excited to eat here tonight."

"I actually picked this place because I remembered you saying you traveled with your dad to Miami and fell in love with rice and beans."

I nodded my head and smiled, doing my best to hide my blushing. After all this time had passed, I wondered what else he remembered.

"But wow. You're so impressive. Doing all of that with your daughter? I can barely make it out of the house alive with both of mine."

"You have two girls? Tell me about them."

His face lit up. "Yes, I do. Twins, actually. They're five. And they both keep me very busy, but I wouldn't trade them for anything in the world."

"Agreed. And believe me, Peyton is a handful."

He chuckled. "She actually has said the same about you."

We shared a laugh that felt familiar.

The waiter arrived with a chilled bottle of wine and filled my glass. When he went over to fill Zaire's glass, he declined and took a drink of his water.

"Oh, I'm sorry. Are you not a fan of Merlot?"

"No, it's not that. I don't drink anymore, actually." He cleared his throat. "Do you remember my brother Eden?"

I nodded my head. "Yes, vaguely, but I remember you saying you were always at odds with him."

"Yeah, well, he ended up in rehab and really turned his life around. We became pretty close after that, and I stopped drinking alcohol around him so he wouldn't be tempted, and that pretty much led to cutting it out altogether."

"I remember you being kind and thoughtful and selfless. The guy who apologized to everyone in line because he didn't want them to think he was skipping, and the guy who picked up ride tickets and gave them to a random boy and girl."

He looked at me in the way that only he could, and this time, I couldn't hide my blushing.

"What happened to you? Why didn't you reach out or respond any of the times I called?"

I took a sip of my wine, unsure of how to answer his question. I could give him the truth, but the truth wasn't pretty…and it was also painful. Still, I didn't want to start things off with half-truths.

"That night, I stayed in the room with my father until the nurses told me they had to wrap him up. And as they wrapped him, every part of me unraveled at the realization that he was gone. The next two weeks, I walked around as an empty shell, and I only made it because I had to plan his home going. Every day, it shocked me and even made me angry that life was still happening. I had to speak with his estate attorney, clients, florist, and realtors, and their presence reminded me that outside, people were still carrying on like the whole world wasn't just split in two."

He nodded and reached over to grab my hand.

"After the funeral, I was alone. No close relatives, no siblings, and no parents. And that reality drained the remaining life inside of me. I lay in bed every day for about a month. The rest of that year was pretty dark. I dropped out of school and made extremely unhealthy choices. Then, one day, a man named Robert and his wife knocked on the door.

"They explained how they were friends and met in the hospital the day I was born. The same day my mother died. And they knew something had to be off because they had a tradition of writing letters and sending pictures back and forth. They connected me with a counselor to help me sort through my grief. They offered me to stay with them in the state they live in, but instead, I decided I wanted to go back and finish school. We kept in contact for a while, but in moving around so much I lost their info. I tried searching for them on Facebook but couldn't find them. Anyhow, to make a super long story short, I didn't respond because I couldn't. Even with counseling, I was grieving for a really long time. Then, I got pregnant that final semester and decided that I shouldn't. And every day after that felt like it had been way too long. I know that isn't much of a—"

"No, it is. I get it. And I've lived enough life to know that even the parts I don't understand work out for my good. I'm really sorry about your dad…and your mom. You've been through so much, and to go through that alone."

He handed me his handkerchief for the tears I didn't even realize were swelling up on the inside.

I dabbed my teary eyes and then started laughing. "Who

the heck still carries around a handkerchief? Are we in a movie?"

He smirked. "Well, it came in handy today, didn't it?"

We ordered our food and, as we waited, caught up on smaller details. His favorite color was now green, and mine was still black. We were both now thirty-three. He got his bachelor's in English literature and a graduate degree in theology. He explained he knew he was supposed to be a teacher after volunteering at a high school in the inner city. I shared that I double majored in chemistry and statistics and that while in the graduate program for genetics, I found out I was pregnant and couldn't work with the materials we used any longer. I spoke briefly about Eddie and his nearly nonexistent relationship with his daughter. After having Peyton, I did go back to work at a lab for a short while, but by then, I knew deep down my passions and focus had changed. I enrolled at a community college to practice and sharpen my art skills. I showed him pictures of some of the pieces I made and sold while traveling.

"I always imagined that you were pretty good, but these are amazing." He continued swiping through my album.

"Thank you."

"No, seriously. The girls would love something like this in their room." He showed me a picture of a mural I created. It was a colorful piece filled with flowers, birds, and butterflies.

"I would like that. Just let me know when."

He handed me back my phone and I stuffed it back inside my tiny purse.

"So, about your daughters…are you and their mother not together anymore, or are you divorced?" I asked with genuine curiosity.

"Widowed."

I raised my hand over my mouth. "Oh my gosh. I'm so sorry."

"Thank you. It's been a while now." He looked off into the distance as if recalling a memory. "It was a few months after the girls were born. Her sister had flown into town, and she wanted a girls' night out to get back to herself. On the way home from the night out with her sister, she was hit by a drunk driver. When I made it to the hospital, she was still in critical condition but thankfully had regained consciousness…"

I reached over this time and grabbed his hand.

"As soon as she saw me, she told me to take out my phone and make a list. I needed to learn how to do the girls' hair. I had to make sure they knew periods weren't gross and that they were natural. She made me promise to give them the real sex talk when they were of age. A few other things like that, but mainly to make sure they knew how much she loved them. I didn't question it; I just knew. She said that if love was enough, she would be here, and we would grow old and gray together." He paused briefly. "She said that she wanted me to be happy and not to mourn her for too long. She passed later that next morning. Thankfully, her sister decided to stay a little longer than planned because the next few months were the most difficult I'd ever experienced: becoming a widow, mourning my wife, and learning to be a single dad at the same time."

I handed him back his handkerchief. "I think you need this now."

He used it to wipe the tears that rolled down his cheek. "Is it a bad sign that we both ended up crying on the first date?" He chuckled forcefully.

Still holding his hand. "We both lived a lot of life in between us knowing each other. I think this was a good place for us to start…so I say this was good, actually."

"I do, too."

CHAPTER 6

Zipporah and I spent so much time talking, sharing stories, and laughing that I ended up forgetting about the plans I made for us to visit an emerging artist gallery, and I was fine doing so as long as she kept smiling.

My phone chimed, and I reached inside my pocket to retrieve it. "I'm sorry. I don't want to miss this in case it's my sister. She's watching my girls tonight."

She nodded her head. "No, absolutely. I understand."

I chuckled and handed my phone to her. "This is a picture of my girls and their aunt. Apparently, they are making cupcakes tonight, and Hope, my oldest, is covered in the batter."

She grabbed my phone, and her eyes widened and she looked back and forth from the image to me.

"What? What is it?"

"I *know* these girls. I just can't believe these are your girls."

"Really? Where do you know them from? Oh…you're Ms. Z, the art teacher!" Now, my eyes widened.

"I am! This is so crazy. Small world, huh?"

I smiled and shook my head, silently asking God what He was up to. What she attributed to the world being small, I knew was truly His perfect timing and sense of humor.

"Hope and Grace have been badgering me non-stop to get to know their art teacher. They both say you're as pretty as a princess."

She blushed again, for the third time tonight. This woman was going to stop my heart altogether.

"Awww, they're sweet. You did an amazing job with them because they're the most polite children I've ever met. I should've known they were yours when I saw them split their snack to give another child who was still hungry extra."

"Thank you. I appreciate you saying that. And Peyton is brilliant. I had to pull some books from my sophomore curriculum because she's so well-read. By the way, your opinions on *The Odyssey* are noted."

She laughed and covered her mouth. "Oh my gosh. Did she really tell you everything I said?"

"I can't be sure if it was everything, but the words 'Eurocentric' and 'sexism' came up, among other things."

"Well...am I wrong?" She arched her eyebrow and twisted her mouth in a way that was enticing.

I cleared my throat. "No, you're not wrong…but still, I don't think I totally agree."

We continued on that way for the remainder of our dinner. It was as if no time had lapsed in the way our conversation slipped right past awkward. For a moment, I felt the guilt rushing back towards me in waves, threatening to carry me away. If no time had passed…. What did that make of the years I cherished with Melissa?

Her phone alerted, and she looked at the screen. "That's Peyton. She sent me a throw-up emoji and a heart-eyes emoji, wanting me to let her know how it's going. She's going to lose it when she realizes you're the twins' father."

She looked at me with those big honey-colored orbs and smiled effortlessly, hopeful. She dared me once to jump with her; I smiled back at her and decided to jump.

"Well, let's head over to them. My girls are also going to be so excited if they're not already asleep."

We made our way out of the restaurant after I covered the bill. While holding the door open for her, I got a glimpse of her curves and shapely features as she walked past me. She was always attractive to me, but the dress she decided to wear tonight had to have been sewn together while on her body.

I let out an exasperated breath. "Jesus, give me strength."

ALL THINGS BEAUTIFUL

***

Our car ride fell into a comfortable silence, and even though there wasn't any music playing, she was humming, nodding her head, and moving her shoulders, and at that moment, it was evident she was the song I wanted to be listening to.

I reached over to the middle console and held my hand open for hers. To which she agreed, and this time we held hands not to comfort one another, but simply to share closeness.

She turned over to me with a delighted look on her face. "Thank you for tonight. I had a really great time."

"Thank you for deciding to come and share your time with me. What made you change your mind?"

"What do you mean?"

"What made you decide to accept my offer and go out with me?"

Her expression perked up. "Peyton, actually..." Her beautiful lips curved into a proud smile. She continued, "It's not because I didn't want to or anything like that. It's just that Friday nights are sort of our thing. We have a standing spa date and watch movies; it's a whole thing." She waved her hands around as if dismissing her previous statement.

"Ohhh. I gotcha. It's a girls' night. We can find some other day of the week to spend time together."

"Oh? Is that your way of asking me out on a second date, Mr. Timothy?"

I pulled into Nicole's driveway and parked the car. I got out and went around to open her door. Even in the dark, her skin was still golden.

"I wasn't planning on asking you so informally as I did over text. But I would love to go out with you again. If you'd have me, Ms. Smith."

Once on Nicole's porch, she looked up at me and inched close enough for me to be intoxicated by her sweet smell and completely captured by her eyes. Everything about her was beautiful, even the way she still chewed on her lip when she was nervous. I wanted to kiss her or even hug her, but I knew better than to do either of those things while she looked that good wearing that dress.

"We should probably get inside. I'm sure either my girls are exhausted, or Nicky is."

"Oh…oh. Yeah, you're probably right." She chewed on the corner of her lip.

"Listen, you should know that…"

I turned to face the door as the sounds of the bolts being unlocked started, followed by the door swinging open.

"You didn't text me back, Mommy!" Peyton stomped and folded her arms around her chest, wearing a multicolored unicorn onesie.

"I'm sorry, Sweet P. I forgot." Zipporah bent down and kissed her daughter before pinching her nose.

"So, how was it? Did you kiss? Did you fall in love all over again? Nicole and I have a bet going on."

"Peyton," Zipporah whispered and shut the door a little so I could be fully seen.

Peyton almost jumped. "Hey…um, hi. Hi, Mr. Timothy. I didn't expect you to still be here."

I cleared my throat. "That's all right. Hi, Peyton. I'm sorry about stealing your mom during your movie night. It won't happen again."

She let out a stiff laugh and began to also chew on her lip. Before she could respond, Nicole came to the front door holding the hand of a very sleepy Hope.

Nicole's face turned pink, and her smile widened as her eyes flickered back and forth between Zipporah and me.

"This is *him*? There's absolutely no way; this is my brother-in-law!" She smiled, looking at Zipporah, and then faced me. "And you! You didn't tell me you were going out on a date. This is my neighbor. The woman I've been wanting you to meet! How crazy is that?"

Hope rubbed her eyes and held up her hands signaling for me to carry her. "Daddy!"

I reached down and picked her up, following the ladies inside.

"How were the girls? Did they give you any trouble?"

Nicole shook her head, eyes still wide with excitement. I could tell she was bubbling up on the inside.

"We were no trouble, Daddy. We were really good girls. Right, Titi Nicky?" Hope asked, picking up her head from my shoulder.

"The bestest," Nicole confirmed.

"You're H & G's dad?" Peyton asked with a hint of disbelief in her voice.

"I am. How old did you think I was?"

Everyone giggled, stealing glances at one another, speaking in code.

I could tell that my presence was killing the mood and that I needed to get out of there soon so they could properly debrief.

"Let me go and get Grace." I walked down the hall and into the spare bedroom where my daughters often slept whenever they spent the night.

Nicole had dedicated her only extra bedroom out of

her two-bedroom condo to my girls. She had no idea how appreciative I was to have her in my life, as well as in the lives of my children.

"Gracey, wake up, baby. It's time to go." I rubbed her back as she shifted around and woke up.

"Hi, Daddy." Grace yawned. "Is P still here? She's my new best friend after my sister."

"She's my best friend, too, Daddy. She's so cool, and look, she painted our nails."

Hope swung her foot across my chest and almost into my face and wiggled her purple toes. Grace threw off the covers she was underneath to show me her pink toes.

"Wow! So beautiful!"

I had learned over the years that everything was a big deal to them, especially when it came to beautification. I made sure to try my best to pay attention to the things they liked.

I picked Grace up with my left hand after shifting Hope over my right shoulder. Once both girls were secured, I walked back towards the kitchen and overheard the hushed whispers come to an abrupt stop.

"As always, thank you, Nicky." I hugged her as much as I could with each girl on one shoulder.

"Don't mention it, Z."

"Have a good night, Peyton. And thank you for painting the girls' nails. They both love it."

"It was fun." Peyton smiled. "Good night, H & G."

Hope and Grace both shot up and sang in unison, "Good night, P!"

"Ms. Z!" Hope squeaked. "You look so beautiful."

"I like your hair, Ms. Z. Daddy, can you do my hair like that?" Grace asked.

"Let's do three ponytails first, okay, Gracey?"

"Thank you both so much." Zipporah smiled.

"They're both right, though. You look beautiful, and I really enjoyed myself with you tonight."

She looked at me and smiled the widest smile I think I'd ever seen on her face before, and then she smirked. "You were with me. Of course, you did."

Her smile was confident and bashful in a way only she knew how to be. Her smirk was coated in the fondness of familiarity that can't be erased with time. A wave of emotion laced over me. Was I attracted to her? Wildly. Did I find everything about her interesting? Compellingly so. Was I unsure of what the road ahead of us looked like? Yes. Yet, right there, I knew I was also deeply in love with her.

I kissed her on her cheek, feeling the heat rise in both

her face and mine. Not caring of all the whooping and awes coming from the small crowd.

"Goodnight, New. I'll call you in the morning."

I strapped both my girls in once in the car before getting in myself and heading home.

"Daddy, if you kissed the princess, does that mean you're a prince?" Grace bubbled.

"Yes, Daddy. You're a prince now!" Hope proclaimed.

The girls fell into a giggle fit and started to deliberate what that made them if I was a prince.

"Daddy, is Ms. Z our new mommy now?" Hope yawned.

I stilled in my seat. What did this make us? How do I explain this to the girls? How do I do any of this without erasing the memories I so badly want them to remember but I know were impossible for them to have?

"No, it doesn't work like that. Ms. Z and I are finding out if we want to…" I paused briefly, trying to pick my words carefully. "If we want to be a family."

"That means she would be our mommy, Daddy. That is how it works. If you get married, she's our mommy," Grace confirmed.

"Daddy's going to get married! Daddy, you have to marry her," Hope agreed.

"I think it's bedtime, girls. But we can talk about it more in the morning."

CHAPTER 7

"Ultimately, it's up to you, Sweet P. I have a few concerns that I'll iron out with your dad if you decide to go. But if you decide you don't want to, I'll just tell him I don't feel comfortable with it."

"Thanks, Mommy. I think I'm going to go…I just really want to think about it first."

I prayed for Eddie to be more active in Peyton's life. I thought that would mean he would call more than just once every few weeks and come to visit for holidays and birthdays instead of just mailing over money and gifts. I did not expect him to call this morning and invite Peyton to stay with him and his long-term girlfriend, Imani. Then again, I was learning that I wasn't in control of how and when God answered prayers.

"Mom, can we take another stop? I want to take a picture of the river."

There were days when sadness, without much warning, and uncontrollably, decided to come for a visit. Today, I woke up thinking of all the things I wish I had gotten to do with my dad, all the things I wish he was still here to see. Peyton sensed this sadness and decided it was time for us to go out on an adventure, as she called it.

I started to slow down my peddling and ease on the brakes of our tandem bike. We decided to spend our Saturday afternoon biking to the Chattahoochee River. It was enjoyable still being able to adventure together stateside in our new home.

We both got off our seats, and I leaned our bike against a tree while Peyton started snapping photos with her phone. We took turns taking photos of each other and a few together.

I had so many photos and memories built with my dad over the years. Even now, with it being years since I've seen him, I still remember the sound of his voice, and the lessons he thought I wasn't listening to were all still etched on my heart. He made up for what I missed with my mother because she wasn't able to. Eddie, on the other hand, was, and late as it was sure, it was still an effort.

"I think you should go." I sat on a rock and crisscrossed my legs. "I still want you to think about it and make a decision you feel good about, but I do think you should go."

Peyton stuck her phone in her pink and neon green fanny pack. Only she could make hiking gear fashionable. She leaned against the rock. "Say more things."

"Well, it'll give you a chance to get to know him without

me around. You both can build a relationship together on your own terms. And you never know; you might find out you actually like him."

"He's my dad. Of course, I love him."

"I'm sure you love him, Sweet P. That doesn't mean you like him, though."

She scrunched her face together before taking a drink of water. "Hmmm…that's a good one, Mom. Can I use that for my practice?"

"For a fee."

While sharing a laugh, her phone rang. She answered it, and I could see Jasmin and Paige's faces on the screen. I said hello to both of them before jumping off the rock to make a phone call of my own.

"Hey, New. How's your bike ride going?" I could hear his handsome grin through the phone.

I never considered myself to be a romantic in any way. I definitely wasn't the swooning or blushing type, at least not in my history. This man, however, had me feeling things entirely too fragile and foreign.

"It's going well." I looked over to Peyton, who was still on FaceTime with her friends. "We're taking a phone call break, apparently. How's your morning going?"

"Pretty good. I'm packing an overnight bag for Hope

and Grace. My in-laws came over for breakfast, and one thing led to the next, and the girls were able to weasel their way into spending the night with their grandparents."

I laughed. "I can imagine it being hard for anyone to say no to them. They're just too sweet and adorable."

"Believe me, I know. But it does mean that I now have an opening. I would love to be able to see you again. Does tonight work for you?"

"I don't think so. I'm not sure what Peyton is getting into…"

I briefly considered leaving Peyton home alone. She was responsible, she knew all the emergency numbers, and I did trust her.

"Actually…" I changed my mind. "I'm open to doing something with you tonight. As long as I don't have to wear heels again. I need a break."

"Noted." He laughed. "Okay then, Zipporah. I have to go now, but I'll come by to pick you up at six."

We said our goodbyes and hung up the phone. I put my phone in my backpack and picked up our tandem bike. Peyton was now sitting on the rock and looked deep in thought with both of her eyes closed.

"Hey, Sweet P. Let's head out before traffic picks up."

Peyton opened her eyes and slid down the rock. She

fixed her pink leggings and swung her legs over her bike seat.

"Is everything okay? You looked far away for a second there."

"Yeah. I'm okay, Mom. I was praying for Jasmine's older brother. It's just a lot going on right now."

"Okay. Is *he* okay?"

"I don't know. But I'm hoping he will be."

We started pedaling the bike and making our way out of the park. I decided not to push any further. Peyton was always open with me, and I knew if she needed something from me, she would come to me.

***

"Please do not hesitate to go next door to Nicole if you need anything at all, okay?"

"Yes, Mom. I won't answer the door for strangers, and I won't burn the house down, either. I'm perfectly capable." Peyton flipped her hair and pushed her glasses up the bridge of her nose. She wore glasses strictly because she wanted to appear more studious, not because she needed them.

"I'll see you later, okay?" I rubbed her hair before planting a kiss on her forehead. "I love you."

"I love you, too, Mommy. Is your location on?"

"Yes, it's on. I'm the mom, remember?"

"When you're going out with your boyfriend, *I'm* the mom." Peyton winked.

"Yeah, yeah. He's not my boyfriend." I turned around the way I had gotten used to modeling for her. "How do I look?"

I was wearing a cream sweatpants set and blue and yellow sneakers. Much more sporty than Peyton would've preferred, but right up my alley.

She held up both thumbs and forced a smile. "It'll do."

"Whatever, dude." I made my way towards the front door, unlocked it and locked eyes with a gorgeous hazel pair. "Hi," was all I managed to say before he pulled me into his strong chest with both arms.

My words could duel with him all they wanted, but my body always relented to his beckoning when around him. I wrapped my arms around the small of his back and completely gave in; for just a minute, I could let him shoulder the weight of my world, especially on a day like today. I felt him bury his face into my freshly washed curls like he always did whenever we were this close. I always wondered if he enjoyed the smell of my hair products and oils.

I continued to hold onto him, not wanting this fluttery feeling replacing the sad to end.

"Hiii, Mr. Timothy," Peyton interrupted before looping a possessive arm around mine.

He cleared his throat and took a small step away from me. "Hi, Peyton. How are you?"

"I'm well, actually. And yourself?"

"I can't complain, thank God." Zaire gave me a weird look before bending down and picking up an arrangement of yellow flowers. "I did get these for you, though."

"Those are really pretty, but my mom doesn't like flowers," Peyton quipped.

She was right, but where was all of this sass coming from? I turned to face her fully a little unsure of how to settle this, and still wanting to have this conversation, whatever this was privately.

"They're actually for you, Peyton," Zaire remarked.

"Really?" Peyton's voice softened. "Thank you, Mr. Timothy." She walked away, holding the bouquet.

"This was extremely kind of you, Old, but would you just give us a moment, please?"

I pushed the door softly before following Peyton into the kitchen.

"Hey, that seemed a little rude, dude. Are you sure you're okay with me leaving?"

"Yeah, I'm fine. Go, Mommy." Peyton hugged me, and her stature seemed softer.

I gave her one final look before leaving, hoping that she really was okay.

***

"How did you know I didn't like flowers?" I asked in between slurps of my giant milkshake.

Zaire brought us to an adult bowling alley and arcade. The interior of the venue was dimly lit and was uniquely draped in velvet curtains. We played two rounds of bowling, where while the score was close, he still technically won. Followed by a round of table hockey, where I won.

"I'm not sure if it's something I remembered or not; I just had a gut feeling that wasn't your thing. I pretty much took a wild guess about Peyton, though. Did she like them?"

"She loved them. That was a good call and really thoughtful of you."

He looked at me in a way that made me feel both illicitly exposed and masterfully seen.

"What is it?"

He laughed awkwardly. "Nothing. I didn't realize I was staring." He let out another laugh and reached for my hand, causing that same fiery feeling. "How is it that you look more beautiful tonight than you did yesterday?"

"Aww, thank you." I blushed. "I do remember making a move and feeling slightly rejected, though, when we made it over to Nicole's." I pinched my fingers together.

He dropped his face in his hands and sighed. "Yeaaah…about that. I in no way wanted to make you feel rejected. You looked amazing, and I am more than just slightly attracted to you. But the dress you were wearing? Maaan. I couldn't have kissed you while you were looking that good."

I blushed again, and this time I covered my face, feeling embarrassed. "Oh my…I'm sorry."

He picked up my face gently and smiled. "Don't be sorry. Again, you looked amazing. I'm sure there will be other times when you look just as appealing. But in those times, I'm going to refrain from kissing you and whatever else I might need to make sure I'm being respectful to God and you and upholding my boundaries."

"What do you mean by boundaries?"

It's not that I'd never heard of the term, I just wanted to know what were his specifically.

"Well, I guess this is a good segway in something I've been meaning to ask you. I'm a believer, and I believe in Jesus Christ. Part of my belief is that my body is a temple, and with that, I don't want to dishonor God by having sex before marriage. And that means I have boundaries to make sure I don't get close to dancing on that line."

I nodded my head in silence, not quite sure if I fully understood.

"Are you also abstinent? But more importantly, are you also Christian?"

"I've been practicing abstinence for the better part of eleven years now," I revealed with a brute laugh. "It wasn't for a higher purpose or anything like that, though, if I'm being truthful. I would like to say I'm Christian. While in Spain, we stayed in the home of a woman who went to church religiously every Sunday. She would share different stories of the Bible with Peyton and me. We decided we would give it a try. And while I pray, the way she taught us to pray, the way I remember my dad praying…I'm not really sure if that makes me a Christian. And I'm not sure if I know all the rules."

"I wouldn't say it's rules, exactly. While, yes, there are clear black-and-white rules, what God desires more than anything is a relationship with us. As that relationship with Him grows, He changes you, and then you find yourself following all the, for lack of a better word, rules."

"So, does that mean I'm a Christian?"

"If you accept and believe Him in your heart and confess that 'Jesus is Lord,' then yes."

We spent the rest of the night talking about what it meant for Jesus to be Lord over my life. He explained that I also needed to believe that Jesus died for my sins and rose from the dead and is now alive. He shared his testimony and how he came to accept Jesus as his personal Savior and that even though he grew up in a believing household, it was still a decision he had to make for himself. The more he talked and explained, the more I found myself having questions about God.

"Do you think my dad is in heaven? I find myself thinking about that quite often, and I'm not sure. I would like to think that he is…but what if he isn't?"

I watched closely as he maneuvered his way into an answer that would be both gentile and honest.

"I'm not sure. I don't think I knew him well enough to say that. But I don't think I could confidently say that about most people. God is our judge, and ultimately, we will all have to hold an account to Him."

I swiped the tear before it could leave my eye. While I fully believed my dad was in heaven, all this conversation just reminded me that he wasn't here.

"Would you and Peyton come to church with me and my family tomorrow? My mom usually makes dinner on Sundays; you both are welcome to come over after the gathering for that, too," he offered.

"I will actually take you up on that."

While I was still learning about my newfound faith, if I could even fully call it that yet, I was curious. I had heard people say that Jesus heals and takes away pain. I was open to trying anything that gave me hope that I could someday be unstuck.

***

"I usually go to the 8 a.m. service with my family..." Zaire started telling me more about his church, but at the sound of 8 a.m., my face turned into a scowl. "But tomorrow, we can catch the 10:30 a.m. service," he finished with a laugh.

"That sounds about right." I laughed in return. "Do I have to wear something specific?"

"No, you don't. Some people wear dresses and suits, and some people wear jeans. I usually wear a hoodie and jeans."

"Okay, perfect. I'm a little nervous. Is that weird?"

"I don't think—hey. Were you expecting guests?" Zaire stammered as he pulled into my driveway.

I turned around from him and looked out the window. I counted two bikes and one skateboard sprawled out near my front door.

"Umm…no. Isn't it past nine?" I shrieked, unbuckling my seat belt and flying out of the car before Zaire could even park.

I sprinted to the front door and found it already slightly opened. I rushed inside finding almost all the lights on and a trail of varying snacks leading to Peyton's bedroom. I twisted the knob of her bedroom door to find it locked.

"Peyton!" I yelled at the top of my lungs.

I heard various hushed whispers and scattering around. Peyton soon after opened the door. Jasmine and Paige both scurried out of the room, followed by a teenage boy who I could only hope and pray was a teenager because he was taller than me.

"Well, hello, girls and boy. When I said my door is always open, I meant as long as I was home," I said, looking at both Jasmine and Paige.

"Hi, Ms. Smith. I'm sorry about how late it is," Paige offered in a soft voice.

"Hi…Mr. Timothy?" Jasmine sounded like she tasted the words as they came out of her mouth and was uncomfortable with how it tasted.

Zaire was now inside, standing by the door.

"Hey, Mr. Timothy! See you Monday," the teenager croaked with a voice that had so much base I almost jumped.

"Bye, Peyton. I can't thank you enough." He waved.

My expression must've matched my inward seething and disapproval because after looking at me, he lowered his face and continued walking outside.

Zaire closed the door after they left.

I shifted my weight and turned toward Peyton, who now had her arms folded across her chest.

"Mom! Did you absolutely have to embarrass me like that? And then why would you bring *him* in here? Now, everyone's going to be talking about it on Monday."

"Peyton, my patience with you is wearing thin today." Even as the words left my mouth, they felt uncomfortable. This wasn't Peyton and me. Maybe it was other mothers and daughters, but it wasn't us. I inhaled and exhaled. "What is going on? This is the first time you've ever been home alone. What made you think it was okay to have people over without asking me first? And who was the grown man in here? Yeah, let's start with that one."

"That's Austin, Jasmine's older brother. I told you I was praying for him earlier."

"That doesn't explain why he was here. In your bedroom. Behind a locked door at that." Now, I folded my arms across my chest.

"Mom, that would be breaking client confidentiality."

"You are not a licensed therapist! I'm inclined to call Jasmine's parents if I don't get some answers."

"Mom, I can't tell you that." Peyton sounded like she was choking on tears.

I didn't know how to move forward, but I did know that I needed answers.

I held out my hand. "Give me your phone."

"Mom."

"Give it to me so I can call Jasmine's mom," I reiterated.

"Mommy, please!"

"Somebody's about to tell me something. It's either going to be you, Austin, or Jasmine's mother, somebody."

"*Oh my gosh, Mom!* He's self-harming! There! Are you happy now?" she snapped.

"Why would I be happy about that? That's ridiculous. I know this was a fun thing at first, but there isn't any client confidentiality when a person is harming themselves, and a real counselor would know that!"

"Wow. You're supposed to be the 'cool' mom. You're supposed to be rational and the kind of mom that listens, unlike Jasmine's mom." She handed me her phone. "There! Now, call her and break confidentiality and risk potentially maybe even making things worse," she snapped again with tears now streaming down her face.

I swallowed the lump that had now formed in my throat. I realized I was also now choking on tears.

"And it's *imminent* harm. I Googled it. He would have to be in imminent harm, but I'm not a *real* counselor, so what would I know?" She walked into her room and shut the door.

There wasn't a manual on how to raise a smart mouth, fearless, dive-in-head-first, sassy, miniature version of yourself. Peyton and I had discussions several times where I had to give her a consequence for something she had done contrary to what I asked her to do, but even then, we always ended in a place of understanding.

I looked over to Zaire, who was still standing by the door.

"I'm sorry about this. You can stay if you want, but I really need to go and talk to her first."

He nodded his head, and I made my way inside Peyton's room.

CHAPTER 8

I watched Peyton's closed bedroom door for what felt like hours. I could overhear Peyton crying, then both of them fussing, followed by more crying.

After a while, I started thinking about my daughters. I knew Austin to be an extremely respectful and, yes, sometimes devious young man. Still, he maintained solid grades and was active in school. With all that being said, I don't know how I wouldn't have kept him in a headlock myself until I got answers if roles were reversed.

I was certainly going to need more help in the future years. But thankfully, to my knowledge, my girls were only interested in princesses and puppies, and I could only pray that would last deep into adulthood.

I walked around the open parts of New's home. Every wall was either painted in something colorful or abstract. Walls that weren't painted had framed paintings or photos on them. The furniture and decorations were bright colors that all worked well together. Her home was lively and vibrant, like an extension of herself.

I sat on the couch and scrolled through my phone. My in-laws had sent photos of the girls shopping. I shook my head and laughed to myself.

I heard the door creak open, and before I could stand up. Zipporah came into the living room where I was sitting and sat in my lap, facing me. She nuzzled her smooth face close to my neck and wrapped her arms around my back. We were going to need to have another conversation about boundaries, but tonight, I held and rocked her as she sat silently.

***

I stretched my arms and yawned; it took my eyes a few seconds to register the room. I looked at my watch, which informed me it was two o'clock in the morning. Apparently, I had fallen asleep with Zipporah still in my lap, also fast asleep.

I couldn't feel my legs, and as peaceful as she looked sleeping, I almost considered not waking her, but I also had to use the restroom.

"New, I need you to get up." I shook my legs underneath her, unable to restrain the involuntary movement as the urge to urinate increased.

Slowly, she woke up and directed me to the restroom.

Afterward, I found her in the kitchen, sitting at the island.

"Good morning." I went to the barstool where she was

and hugged her.

"Good morning, Zaire. Thank you for staying, but I'm sure you're exhausted. I know I am."

I yawned and nodded my head, bringing my arms up for a deep stretch. "I am. How is everything? Between you and Peyton, I mean."

She yawned and threw her head back. "She's just so brave." She shook her head and laughed softly. "I remember my dad saying that about me his whole life. However, with me, I jumped off cliffs into rivers for fun. She's deeply sensitive, intuitive, wanting to help and heal everyone, kind of brave. No idea where she got that from."

We both shared a laugh. I remember her telling me years ago that she didn't have many friends and didn't consider herself to be a people person. She thought I was crazy for being her friend, and I guess I was. Crazy about her.

"If it's any relief, I'm hanging on by a thread with my girls most days. They used to be so much easier and could care less if they were wearing a matching pair of shoes. Now, as they get older and more opinionated, they want more. They let me know exactly what they want to wear, how they want their hair, and I get an earful when I can't pull it off just right."

"Sounds like we should team up." She laughed.

"Maybe we should."

ALL THINGS BEAUTIFUL

We stared at each other silently, allowing the weight of our words to settle.

"I should get going." I yawned. "I can be back here at ten for service if you're still coming."

"Okay. See you then." She yawned and walked me towards the door.

***

"Yeah, I learned so much, and the teachers were really nice. Thank you for inviting us, Mr. Timothy."

I looked over my shoulder at Peyton. "For sure. I'm glad you enjoyed the teen ministry."

I was still figuring out the rhythm of my relationship with Peyton. It seemed like she was excited for me to be dating her mom, but yesterday, I felt anything but excitement coming my way. Today, on the other hand, she seemed pleasant enough. I wanted her to be comfortable with me but wanted to go at her own pace.

"What did you think of the gathering?" I looked at Zaire, who was still flipping through pages and reading the Bible I purchased and had engraved for her earlier this morning.

"It was so good! He really broke down the scriptures so well. I even took notes on my phone.... Thank you, Mr. Timothy," she said in a sing-songy voice, mimicking her daughter. She winked and blew a kiss at me.

"Mom, don't be gross. I will throw up." Peyton whined.

She looked in the backseat and stuck her tongue out at her daughter, causing them both to erupt in laughter. I couldn't help but imagine what it would sound like, also having my daughters in the mix. I prayed silently that it would sound just as blissful.

"Okay, we're here." I got out of my car and opened the door for both Peyton and Zaire.

"Wow. This home is resplendent. It looks like we've just stepped into a page of *Architect Digest*." Zaire shared.

I held onto her hand and gave it a slight squeeze. I didn't want her getting into her head about meeting my parents.

Peyton held on to Zaire's free hand. I shrugged it off and charged it to her feeling nervous, but part of me then wondered if I had entered into a secret competition.

I used my key to unlock the door and held it open for Peyton and Zaire. I called out for my parents and heard my mom's slippers sliding across the wood-paneled floor towards us.

"Hey, Mom." I hugged her and kissed her on the cheek.

"Hey, cutes. I missed you." She looked over to Zipporah and her daughter with a welcoming smile.

"Mom, this is Zipporah and her daughter Peyton," I introduced.

"Aren't you adorable?" My mother said to Peyton before looking at Zipporah. "You look so familiar. Have we met somewhere before?"

"I'm not sure, but you actually look really familiar, too."

We walked towards the dining room together as they continued trying to figure out where they might've seen each other before.

"Robert, honey, come down quick," my mom shouted. "You have to see Zaire's girlfriend, Zipporah. That's so funny, isn't it? Two Z names."

Zipporah looked at me, and I looked back at her. If she was okay with it, I was. My daughters were already planning our wedding; I was okay with her being my girlfriend.

My mom started tapping on her chin. "What are your parents' names? Maybe I know them."

Zipporah explained, "My mom's name is also Zipporah. She passed away the day I was born. My dad's name is Jeremy. He also passed almost sixteen years ago."

"My Lord! That's what it is—" my mom started to say and was interrupted by my dad announcing his entrance as he walked down the stairs.

As soon as he walked into the dining room, Zipporah's eyes lit up. She turned to my mom and hugged her. "You're

Joyce! I'm so sorry I didn't recognize you earlier." Zipporah sounded like she was crying, and that confused me all the more.

I looked at my dad and greeted him.

He also walked to Zipporah and hugged her, swinging her back and forth. Peyton and I both looked at each other, confused as to what was taking place in front of us.

Zipporah explained that my dad was the Robert she talked about during our first date. My parents were the couple who encouraged her to see a counselor the year after her father's death. My dad explained soon after Z's mother gave birth, she was pronounced dead, and that weighed heavily on her father, as I can imagine. He saw Jeremy stricken with grief, looking through the nursery glass when he felt an urge to approach him. He shared the story, and that led to my father praying with him. He promised Jeremy that even though a really terrible thing just occurred, he still believed God had a plan.

My mother told me a few times when I was younger that she picked my name from a man my father met in the hospital the day I was born. Part of me regretted not being more open with my parents when I was younger. I never shared with them my relationship with Zipporah. I'm sure if I had, so many things would have played out differently. Maybe we wouldn't have been separated for so long. Maybe not at all. I shook my head and got rid of those thoughts of an alternate timeline, one in which I would've never met Melissa.

My father explained they kept in contact over the years because my parents felt strongly led to do so. They sent letters back and forth that included pictures of us. My mom retrieved some of the letters they received from Zipporah's dad. Here my parents were, showing me childhood pictures of the woman I met and fell in love with on a ski lift years ago. There wasn't an awkward moment between them. She fit in like she'd always belonged there. My parents even embraced Peyton, and her interactions with my parents were harmonious. The love between all of them was evident. They spent the night becoming reacquainted and filling in the gaps of the time they'd lost.

When my in-laws dropped Hope and Grace off, it was non-stop laughter and giggles. I could tell my girls already looked up to Peyton and were in complete awe of Zipporah.

It was everything I wanted it to be. What I expected to be an introduction turned out to be a reunion, and that left an achingly empty hole in my chest.

***

"That was a great question, Samantha. Again, class, this assignment will weigh heavily on your first quarter grades, so please let me know if you need anything else cleared up."

I continued to walk around the classroom, answering questions and providing assistance to the students in my eighth-grade class. In the back corner, I noticed a hand flew up. As I walked towards Austin, I noticed his finger was in a brace.

"Hey, Austin. Shoot."

"I just wanted to know if the reference page counts as one of the required pages?" Austin questioned.

I let out a small laugh. "Nice try, but it does not." I then lifted my head and announced, "To be clear, everyone, the assignment needs to be three full pages, not including the title or reference pages."

A few dispersed laughs and groans sounded in the classroom.

Austin smirked. "It was worth a shot. But thank you, Mr. Timothy."

"Absolutely." I pointed at his hand. "Did you jam it? I've been there."

He laughed awkwardly and hid his hand under his desk. "Yeah, something like that."

I recalled Peyton sharing he was self-harming and counted to myself the times I had seen Austin in a splint, brace, sling, or cast on a body part. While I sustained several injuries in school, it was always a result of being on the court, either in practice or a game. I didn't recall, however, Austin ever participating in any sports outside of riding his skateboard.

I felt one of those urges wanting me to speak with him privately but instead decided to spend some time in prayer and get advice on it first. I didn't want to jump in haphazardly, not with something this serious.

At the sound of the bell ringing, the students got up and started to leave the room. I said my goodbyes and found myself intuitively making my way to Austin's seat, unsure of what I was going to say.

"Hey, Mr. Timothy?" he initiated.

"Yes?"

"Are you dating Peyton's mom?"

This was the last thing I was expecting to talk with him about, and not a conversation I planned on having with a student, either.

"I don't think that's appropriate for us to talk about…"

A thought occurred to me that if I wanted him to be honest with me, I might as well lead by example and be honest with him.

"But I am. It's not a secret or anything; it's just new," I admitted.

"Naw, you're good. I won't say anything to anyone." He broke eye contact and started fidgeting with his book bag zippers. "Peyton mentioned that her mom made her tell her…some stuff. Did she tell you about that?"

I sighed. "No, she didn't tell me. I don't think she would do that, but I was there to hear it."

"Oh."

"I told you guys that I used to teach at a middle school in the city, right?"

"Yeah."

"I had a kid in one of my classes during my first year named Bryson. He missed over forty days of school, and whenever he was in school, he would get into a bunch of different fights; he even tried to get at me a few different times. His bike got a flat tire one day after school, and I decided to help him patch it. Long story short, it turned out he had a lot going on at home. And while not everything changed in his home life, I think he realized talking to someone changed a lot of his perspective. That same kid who repeated sixth grade twice is now graduating college next fall. Anyhow, that might mean nothing to you…but I just wanted you to know that there are people you can talk to. Even if that person isn't me."

He nodded, packed his bag, and started heading toward the door.

"Is fifth period still your free period?"

I looked up to find Austin standing by the door.

"It is. I usually go pick up my girls then, but if you let me know ahead of time, I can work something out."

"Okay, I'll let you know."

***

"Congratulations, man! How are you feeling about this?"

"I'm excited, bro! Thank you. I was shocked for like the first two days, but then it hit me that I was going to be someone's father. The thought of that is crazy." Eden shook his head and grinned profusely.

"I get you, man. It still shocks me sometimes myself, and it's been five years, bro."

We both chuckled. Eden shared that he and his wife Daisha were now expecting. She was only a few weeks along, but this explained why she wasn't feeling well a few weeks ago.

"Don't tell Mom and Dad, though. She has this whole thing she's planning on doing to surprise them, and believe me, she's been a little snippy recently." Eden covered his mouth on the screen.

"I heard that!" Daisha yelled from wherever she was,

causing me to almost fall over in laughter.

"I remember that, too. Mel and I felt like enemies in that final trimester. She couldn't even look at me sometimes."

It wasn't often that I said Melissa's name out loud, even while I thought of her often. At first, that was mainly because I couldn't handle reliving her unexpected death; however, it became something sacred, much like the memories of her that were cemented in my mind.

"Where'd you go there?" Eden's voice snapped me back to reality.

"Nothing, just thinking." I shrugged. "When did you say you both would be coming down?"

"End of the week, right, Mamas?" he called over to Daisha, who's face soon filled the screen.

"Yup. We get there Friday night. I think we'll be landing at 7 p.m.," Daisha confirmed.

"Oh, I should be able to pick you both up. The school's Harvest Fest should be finished by then."

Daisha smiled. "Thank you, Z. You should come with your girlfriend; I'm excited to meet her. Eden gave me the run down and it sounds like it's meant to be to me."

Meant to be. As if it was always meant to be. While that should be comforting, it makes me feel like a horrible man.

"Yeah, yeah." I cleared my throat. "I'll see if she can come along."

Daisha, content with my answer, walked away and handed the phone back to Eden, who was now scarfing down the rest of his lasagna.

"Well, all right, bro. Imma leave you to it. I have a few papers that I still need to finish grading."

"Hold up, man. Are you good? You sounded real hurt last week when you thought she was ghosting you. What's up with y'all now?" Eden probed.

"Man." I huffed. "If I'm being perfectly honest with you, nothing is going on. We're good, and she's…she's amazing. But after everything that happened on Sunday…I don't know, man. I've known her since I was twelve. Mom has basically known her since she was born. So many pieces about us just…fit?" I paused for a moment to consider what I really needed to say and hoped it would be received well. "I wanted this. I mean, I prayed for this. But now that it's happening, it feels…I don't know. Wrong? Like it shouldn't be this easy. And as far as Mel, I mean, I don't know. It feels like I'm dishonoring her. I know that probably doesn't make sense, but it feels that way. I don't want to be that guy."

"What guy exactly?"

"The kind of guy who quickly moves on. I don't want

to feel like I'm replacing her. Or treating what we had like it never existed."

"I doubt anyone who was there to witness you mourn your wife, try and hold yourself together for your girls, and raise them alone would call this moving on too quickly. It's been five years, bro. Not five days or even months. And not that time has anything to do with it, but the point is you deciding to pursue her, even eventually marry her, doesn't diminish what you experienced and shared with Mel."

I paused, unsure of how to respond. Unsure if his words, regardless of their truth, were enough to stop me from feeling like I was simultaneously betraying the woman who I vowed to love until my last breath.

He took my silence as an opportunity to continue, "But if you aren't sure you're capable, then don't pursue her. Not to sound too harsh, but Melissa is gone. You loved her and were faithful to her, but now she *is* gone. She's in heaven at perfect peace, and I'm pretty sure she isn't worried about you remarrying. That's reality. Zipporah is here, and she deserves all of you if she's really like what you make her out to be."

"I get that. Believe me, I get that here." I pointed to my head. "Not sure if I get that everywhere else, though."

"Mmmm. I feel you," Eden replied. "It sounds like you don't believe God is good."

"What do you mean?"

"Well, you said you prayed for this. Now that your prayers have been answered, you're worried that it's too easy? It's either you believe God is good or you don't. And as far as Melissa, I can only imagine all the thoughts you're having about that, but you moving on isn't dishonoring her. If a man who finds a wife has found favor with the Lord, you've found favor twice. That's a blessing. Don't rob yourself from experiencing His goodness fully."

"Wow. I didn't think about it that way. Thanks, bro."

"I know, man." Eden laughed, cocking his head back. "I should start charging you."

We spent a moment in prayer together and then continued catching up. I shared some of my concerns about Austin with him, hoping he'd be able to give me advice on how to talk to him. I was grateful to have him to talk all this through with. A few years ago, we barely exchanged more than just a few words to one another, but now I was looking forward to having him in town. I silently thanked God again for His mercy and grace, which was abundant in my life.

CHAPTER 9

"I'm not joking, Eddie. I will be in Los Angeles so fast, and you won't like me much once I'm there."

Eddie raised both of his hands on the screen, symbolizing his surrender and defeat. "I got it. Don't worry, she'll be safe. Imani barely lets me ride my motorcycle anymore. I promise I won't let her get on without a helmet…and that's if we even get on."

I sighed. "Okay. Take her EpiPen with you wherever you go. I've never had to use it, but I always have it."

"Really, Mom?" Peyton leaned into my shoulder while we both sat on the couch and spoke to her father on FaceTime.

"Of course, dude. Just in case." I reached into my purse and pulled out the silver and gray protective tube. "Oh, and the last thing, she sometimes—"

Peyton interrupted me by jumping onto my lap and covering my mouth with both of her hands. "Mommy, I don't want him to know," she whispered.

I nodded my head. "She sometimes wakes up in the middle of the night for a snack. So just have something not too sugary for her to munch on."

She smiled and sat back on her seat cushion, happy that I was able to divert from revealing she still sometimes had accidents during the night time.

"Okay, got it." Eddie made an imaginary check mark with his fingers. I rolled my eyes playfully. "I'm really excited to see you, PeyPey. I have so much planned, and my parents are also going to be in town. We'll drive to Santa Monica, where you can meet my brother and your cousins…" Eddie continued listing off some of the things he had planned for them to do together. While Peyton and I were both still hesitant, I also had high hopes that this would be good for her.

Eddie would be flying into town late Friday and spending the night here. Together, they would fly back to his home in Los Angeles the next morning, where she would be until Thursday during her fall break.

"Mommy! I'm going to see Steven and Stephanie in real life instead of just FaceTime calls." Peyton couldn't control her excitement at that.

I smiled back at her and left the room to allow her to continue talking to her father without me hovering. Once settled on my bed, I dialed Nicole.

"Hey, girlfriend!" she squealed into the line.

I giggled. "Hey, girlfriend."

I had come to look forward to Nicole's pep. We spent a lot more time together since I started working as the art teacher in her after-school arts program. While she was five years younger than me, we clicked in a way I hadn't ever clicked with a friend before.

"Do you have big plans for the weekend with Peyton gone?" I heard rustling in her background.

"No, not really, actually. Zaire mentioned going to a basketball game with his brother on Saturday. So, I'll probably just stay in that day. Oh, and church on Sunday."

"Absolutely not! We should do something. We could go get our nails done, maybe do dinner and drinks. I could invite Daisha, and we make a whole girls' day out of it."

Nicole sounded excited, as she usually did, and I didn't want to burst her bubble. I had only just gotten used to her, and I wasn't sure if I was ready to emerge and become a social butterfly all of a sudden.

"You're thinking…and if you think too much about it, you'll say no. Don't think. Just come. You'll have a good time, I promise. And your drinks can be on me," she protested.

"Okay…okay. It's a date." I gave in.

"Yay! I'm excited." I heard more rustling in her background.

"Are you still at the community center? Do you need help with anything?"

She laughed. "I'm okay…I think. I'm home making some shirts for the kiddos at REACH. I'm just trying to figure out this Cricut."

"I can be there in an hour if you'd like."

"*Yes*, pleaseee," she stressed.

We laughed and exchanged goodbyes.

I walked back out to the living room and found Peyton ending her call with her father.

"Goodbye, Eddie. See you tomorrow." I waved at the screen.

"Bye XYZ. See ya soon."

Peyton ended the call and lay on the couch.

"Do you want to come and help me and Nicole figure out a Cricut?" I asked, walking past her and into the spare bedroom I turned into a makeshift studio.

"Mmm…I don't think I want to have any parts of that disaster in the making." Peyton walked in behind me and plopped herself up on a stool. "What are you working on now?"

"Well, this one is done. I'm just waiting for it to dry before I wrap it and have it shipped." I stepped back, looking deeply into the canvas of the piece I started working on when we moved and had yet to finish. "This one, I'm not sure what it is yet."

The painting being shipped to a woman in Virginia Beach was a painting of a black boy chewing on a piece of pink bubblegum. In her email inquiry, she emphasized how important it was for him to look joyful. The painting beside it, the one I was working on to stay creative and fill in my idle time, was splotches of different colors and one intense splotch of black in the right upper-hand corner of the canvas.

"I can help you figure it out." Peyton got off the stool and stood next to me, tapping her index finger on her chin.

"Hit me. What do you think?"

Since Peyton declared she was a therapist in the making, she had been reading into my personal art projects, saying they were a mirror into my soul.

"Mm…I think you have to finish first. But this part feels sad." She pointed to the black spot on the canvas.

"It does feel sad, doesn't it?" I agreed.

***

"You're all set. How do you like it?" I held the mirror up and faced it towards the nine-year-old boy sitting in my face painting booth at the harvest fest.

"It's so cool. I look just like Spiderman." He got up and ran off with his friends.

I cleaned off my brushes in the cup of water and waited for more kids to show up at my booth.

I imagined when we picked Chestmire Christian Academy it would be a pretentious school, but the Harvest Fest was nothing compared to what I could've imagined. Parents, teachers, and even some students volunteered for different booths or to compete in races, sports, and games. There were so many different food booths it smelled like a carnival. The corn maze had overtaken the entire staff parking lot, and the pumpkin patch was something out of a movie.

Peyton was currently at the dive pit with her friends, trying to dunk their teachers.

"Ms. Z! Ms. Z!"

I looked up from the table to find Old and his daughters racing over to my table.

"Hi, Hope! Hi, Grace! How are you guys?"

They each answered and proceeded to tell me about their day in school. Apparently, some of the kids in their classroom teased them about being the same person and kept purposefully mixing up their names.

"Oh, no! That is not okay!"

"Ms. Z, you have to make a serious face. Right, Daddy?" Grace looked over to Zaire, who was leaning against the tent post, watching the interaction.

He walked closer to us and sat down. "Yeah, let's show her how to make a serious face."

I watched as all three of them scrunched their eyebrows together. I did the same and also puffed out my lips and held air in my cheeks.

"You're so silly, Ms. Z" Hope erupted in laughter, followed by Grace.

I painted a flower on Hope's cheek and a butterfly on Grace's.

"See." I handed them the mirror, and they took turns looking into it. "Now, no one will mix you up."

"What about when it washes off?" Hope asked, sounding defeated.

"Yeah, can we leave it on forever, Daddy?" Grace asked.

He started to shake his head.

"Well, it will eventually wash off. But that doesn't make you the same. You both look very similar, but look…" I pointed at their reflections in the mirror. "Hope, you have loose curls, and Grace, you have a tighter curl pattern. Hope, you have more freckles on your nose. Gracey, you have more freckles on your cheeks. And sure, you both may like a lot of the same things, but you also have some things that are different, right?"

"Yeah! Because my favorite color is pink!" Grace exclaimed. "And Hope's is purple." She pointed at her sister.

"Exactly! Just like that. You're both very different people. As long as you remember that, it doesn't really matter what anyone else thinks."

They looked at each other and giggled together like they were sharing secrets.

"Daddy, can we go to the bounce-y house?" Hope asked.

Zaire looked around and spotted someone who I assumed was a familiar face. He waved at them and sent his girls over to the woman and her small kids, and they all entered the bounce house together.

"Am I next?" Zaire sat down on the bench sitting in front of me.

He shared that he would be playing basketball today. He kept out the part where his toned legs and defined arm muscles would be out on full, glorious display.

"I guess you are." I snapped myself out of my daze and tried to refocus. Even though I would just as easily get lost in the curve of his mouth or his captivating eyes, it was a lot safer than lusting after his body. I picked up my small paint pallet. "What do you want? Most of the boys are getting their favorite superheroes." I teased.

"I'll take whatever you want to give me." He inched closer to me and licked his lips before smiling.

I picked up my brush and started painting army stripes on his face to obscure the fluttering feeling in my stomach.

"Are you enjoying yourself?"

"Do you mean here at the festival? Or here painting your face?"

"I meant the festival." He chuckled. "But you can answer both."

"At the festival, I really am. They really outdid themselves." I felt my lips pulled upward into an instinctive smug. "As far as you go…eh." I held out my hand and shifted it to gesture so-so.

He smiled and started to tickle and poke my sides. I snorted several times while gasping for air. His tickles gripped deeper into the cushion of skin just beneath my ribs. I heard myself getting uncontrollably louder.

"Stop. Please. Stooop," I managed to say in between bouts of laughter.

Without further protest, he stopped. I rubbed my side

and continued laughing. I laughed so hard that tears seeped out of my squinted eyes. The tears of laughter quickly turned into fuller-sized, happier ones. I threw my arms around him without thinking, leaned in, and hugged him. After so many years, since my dad passed, I forgot that I was ticklish.

I looked up at him, sure I looked half crazy laughing and crying at the same time. He looked down at me and absorbed it without asking any questions. As if he knew. As if he understood.

***

"Not only that, but I've had six people ask me today if you're with my English teacher. Six, Mom!" Peyton stressed.

Peyton was currently lecturing me about my "intimate" moment with Mr. Timothy, scarring her and simultaneously ruining her reputation for life.

"Well, did you tell them to mind the business that pays them?" I stuffed a handful of popcorn in my mouth and faced Peyton.

Peyton groaned and stomped her feet. "Mom, this is school. Drama and gossip *do* pay them. It's how we make it through the entire school day."

"So, what you're saying is my tuition dollars are going

towards you gossiping with your friends all day? Noted."

Peyton dug her hand in the popcorn bucket before stuffing her mouth, obviously dissatisfied with my answers.

"Hey, dude." I reached over for her now full cheeks. "I don't care what people think. I care what you think. What happened to him being forever bae? What's going on?"

Her arched brows softened. "Nothing, Mom. I just didn't think forever bae would also be my teacher."

I knew my daughter; she felt a lot more than she was letting on.

Before I could fully process a response, the basketball teams came out to the court, and cheering began. The high school varsity team would be playing against the teachers, who played basketball in either high school or college.

I cheered loudly and clapped my hands. From the stands, I could see Zaire looking around with his cupped hands about his eyes to shield them from the sun. When he spotted us, he pointed in our direction and grinned.

A few people in the crowd turned around to see who he was painting, including a long, dark-haired woman who looked more than just displeased when she looked at me.

Peyton sank into my lap.

"Ohmygoshmomwouldyoujustkillme."

ALL THINGS BEAUTIFUL

I picked her up and squeezed her. "You're right. That was a bit cheesy. I can't promise that he will, but I'll behave this whole game. I promise."

***

"P!" Grace and Hope both sang.

Peyton squatted down and gave them each a high five and a hug. I wasn't yet fully convinced that she was okay with Mr. Timothy, but she already had a sisterly bond with both of his daughters.

"Daddy, can we all go to the pumpkins together? With P and Ms. Z?" Hope asked while Grace nodded her head and smiled eagerly.

I know they both had him wrapped around their minuscule fingers.

"Yeah, that's okay with me, if it's okay with you, Peyton," Zaire responded.

Peyton shrugged, not looking at him. "Sure. Yeah, let's go, H & G." She held onto their hands and led the way, never directly acknowledging him.

I opened my mouth to say something to her, but Zaire nudged me with his shoulder. "So, we didn't win, but we came close. And if I'm being honest, that might be worse than a blowout."

I sensed he wanted to change the topic, and unsure of what to say to Peyton right now, I let him.

"Oh yeah? Why's that?"

"Coming close means we could've won," he said while stretching his arms and lower back, still while walking.

"Oh yeah? You sure about that? You were playing teenagers in their prime. Just be glad you got up when you fell…both times," I teased.

"It's like that? Okay." He threw his head back in laughter before wrapping a sweaty arm around my shoulders.

"No, no. You played well. You and Mr. Washington carried the team."

We continued to walk along the pumpkin patch and talked about everything and entirely nothing. He shared that his brother Eden and his sister-in-law Daisha wanted to meet me, if possible, tonight and asked if I would ride with him to the airport to pick them up. I declined. I told him that with Peyton leaving with her father in the morning for the next few days, we had plans to hang out all night until we both fell asleep.

"They'll be here for a few weeks; there'll be time for you guys all to meet, Lord willing. What's Peyton's theme for tonight?"

I laughed. "Uhhh…. She's still deciding. She said it's

between Barbie and Bratz. And apparently, the two dolls have completely different aesthetics. Go figure."

"I'm not really sure what that means, but I am sure you'll both enjoy it. You both are really good together."

"Yeah? I think so, too."

"Hey." He stopped walking and held onto my hand. "If this ever gets in between what you guys have, let me know, okay? And we'll end it."

I stopped walking now also, unprepared to hear those words. Uncertain of how to respond.

"Daddy, can we go take a pretty picture?" Grace huffed after running towards us with Hope and Peyton following. "See, Daddy? The cameraman is taking pictures." Grace pointed.

"Daddy, can Ms. Z and P get inside the picture?" Hope chimed.

Zaire looked at me first, then at Peyton. He looked just like he did when he was on the ski lift and in the Ferris wheel. Scared. Panicked. Unsure.

He started to rub his neck and croaked, "Girls, we can take a picture, just the three of us, together. I think that'll be okay for today."

"But why, Daddy?" Graze asked, now pouting.

"See, Daddy. It's one, two, three, four, five of us. Let's take a picture *all* together," Hope attested.

I squatted down, prepared to explain to them briefly that maybe we could take a picture together another time.

"We can all take a picture together," Peyton interrupted, shocking me and Zaire equally. "Let's do it, Mom. If that's okay with you, Mr. Timothy."

Zaire cleared his throat. "Yeah? Yeah. Okay…. Let's do it."

Peyton rejoined Hope and Grace and walked towards the stacks of hay and assembled pumpkins. I looked at Zaire and shrugged, also unsure of what was happening.

We did four poses together, again attracting an audience. Peyton opted for us to do a fake laughing pose. Grace suggested we do funny faces for her pick. Hope made us yell boo and look scared for hers. Finally, the photographer had us do a classic family pose.

He had Zaire and me sit on the big haystack in front with Peyton behind us. He placed both Hope and Grace on a side. He told them to each look at us while we looked at each other. We complied.

After completing the corn maze, we made our way out so Peyton and I could pick up Eddie from the airport.

Zaire and I didn't talk much. I assume the heaviness

of our previous conversation was still weighing on him. I never considered Peyton not liking him. I never really thought of anyone besides the two of us in the picture, and now, quite literally, there was a picture with five.

The ball was in our court, Peyton's, if I'm being completely honest. While he also had his own children, they were younger, and they liked me. "Chose me," as he puts it. It was different for him. For us, however, I couldn't see myself being with anyone Peyton didn't like. Regardless of how much I liked them.

We stopped by the picture booth on our way out to pick up the prints. Zaire paid the egregious ten-dollar fee for each picture. Hope and Grace cheered and cooed, pleased with how the pictures turned out.

"I gotta admit, we look good together." I smiled at Zaire, who still looked far off.

As if he was snapped out of a trance, he shook his head and looked at the pictures. "You guys look good." He smiled warmly. "I'm wearing basketball shorts and performance tights."

"Can I see them?" Peyton asked.

Zaire looked up from the photo and handed them to her. "Of course. Here you go."

Peyton looked at the photos intently, flipping between all four poses.

"What do you think?" I asked, chewing on the corner of my lip.

"Yeah, P. Is it pretty?" Grace asked.

"It is really pretty, G," she responded. "We look like we match."

"Yay! P says it's pretty, Daddy." Hope hoorrayed.

I silently sighed in relief, but knowing my daughter, I also knew there was a lot to unpack in that statement. Still, it was something.

CHAPTER 10

"Hey, bro. It's good to see you, man." I got out of the car and clapped hands with my brother before pulling him into a hug.

"I've missed you, lil bro. It's been too long," Eden returned.

I let go of him, turned to his wife, Daisha, and hugged her. "It's good to see you too, sis. Even though you aren't showing yet, you're definitely glowing."

Daisha smiled. "Aww, Z. You're too sweet. Rub off on my husband, please." She squeezed my shoulder and walked over to my car.

"See what I mean, bro? She hates my guts these days." Eden laughed as he opened the passenger door for his wife and helped her in before kissing her.

"I love you, babe. I do. I just also can't stand you at the same time." Daisha smiled sheepishly. "I really don't understand what's going on."

Eden got in the backseat as I buckled my seatbelt.

"I'm pretty sure that means this baby is going to be his twin. Probably just a wives' tale, though; we'll see." I looked back at my brother. "I just hope it is true that this baby is a boy because you'd make an ugly girl."

We all laughed. Eden and I continued to jest with one another for the remainder of the car ride. The last time he was in town was a little over a year ago. Although we spoke frequently, there was something about being with him physically. I only hoped this time, he would be with us for more than just a few weeks.

I arrived at my parent's home, where they would be staying during their visit. My mom prepared a welcome dinner and wanted us to all eat together. I invited Nicole as well. Even though Melissa was no longer with us, I still considered her fully my sister, as did my family.

"Mama, I missed you so much." Daisha hugged my mom and greeted her.

I kissed my mom's cheek and walked into the living room, where my girls were currently on top of my dad's back like he was a horse.

"Girls, Grandpa is old. You might hurt him." I laughed.

At the sound of my voice, both Hope and Grace jumped off his back and into my arms. I kissed them both before placing them down.

"Who's old? Not me, boy. I've still got it," my dad argued while slowly getting off from his knees and into a standing position.

"I almost fell asleep while you were standing, old man." I hugged and kissed my father while he slapped my back and laughed.

I sat on the couch with my father and watched as the girls played with their baby dolls on the floor.

Just then, Eden, Daisha, and my mom walked into the living room. The girls jumped in excitement, and each ran toward their aunt and uncle. I told them this morning that I had a surprise for them after the Harvest Fest; they both swore it was a new toy.

As the girls talked their heads off, trying to recant all the stories and events that had happened since they last saw each other, I checked my phone. I didn't have any missed calls or texts from New. I know I had just seen and spent the day with her, but I already missed her.

I decided to send her a text instead.

> "I miss you. Hope you and Peyton are having a great night."

"And Daddy has a girlfriend who's a princess. She's gonna be our new mommy when they get married. And her name is Ms. Z. And they kissed!" Hope informed proudly.

"No, but Daddy kissed her on the cheek. Not on the lips, so he's not a prince yet," Grace corrected.

ALL THINGS BEAUTIFUL

I looked up to find both Hope and Grace giggling while everyone else's stares made their way over to me.

"You have a mommy, remember Hope?"

I was determined to give Zipporah all the space in my heart that she deserved. I was working out within myself, loving her, being fully aware of God's favor towards me, and not allowing guilt to rob me of this. Melissa still was my wife. She died being my wife. I was learning to make space, but that didn't mean I was trying to find the girls a new mother.

Hope shook her head. "But Daddy, we want a new mommy. A mommy in real life and not a picture mommy. Grandma, tell Daddy we want a new mommy."

"Hey everyone, sorry I'm late." Nicole stumbled in and interrupted. "Mama Joyce, I know you said not to bring anything, but I made a short rib; it's on the table. You know me, and I just couldn't sit still."

"Titi Nicky!" Grace sprang up from Daisha's lap into Nicole's arms.

We took turns greeting Nicole and then sat down for dinner.

My mom made all of our favorites, even though she complained that the dinner didn't "match." She made steak and potatoes for my dad and me. Smothered turkey wings and rice for Eden. Vegan greens, yams, and potato salad for

Daisha. Seafood pasta for Nicole. And whatever she made for dessert was for my girls.

"Mom, this is all really good." I used my napkin to wipe my mouth.

I looked down at Hope and Grace, who were pushing food around on their plates, signaling they were finished eating even though their plates were only half eaten. Chicken nuggets and fries, they could never get enough of, but real food? That was a challenge every other day.

"It is really good, Mom. And this short rib, sis? Bomb." Eden muffled with a full mouth.

Nicole smiled at Eden and then looked over to my mom. "Yeah, Mama Joyce, I know this probably took all day. Thank you so much for having me."

"Thank you, baby. I'm just glad to have you all home. The house is quiet whenever you guys aren't around." My mom looked over to my dad, and he squeezed her hand.

They looked at each other for a moment as if communicating telepathically. Finally, my dad smiled, and my mom soon followed.

I looked over to Eden, who was also watching this strange exchange between our parents.

"Is…everything okay? Mom? Dad?" I asked.

"Yes, baby. Everything is fine. We just missed you

all, and we're so happy you're here. Together," my mom offered. "But where is Zipporah and that sweet girl of hers? I expected them to be coming as well, even though I don't yet know their favorite foods."

"Yeah, Z. I thought she was going to be riding with you to the airport?" Daisha asked while setting down her fork and knife.

"Her daughter, Peyton, is flying to visit her dad in California tomorrow. It's the first time they'll be separated for that long, so they're hanging out tonight…just them."

"She'll be meeting up with us tomorrow, though, Daisha! Girls' night!" Nicole squeaked, holding up her glass.

Daisha laughed. "Good! I'm excited to meet her. And honestly, just for some much-needed girl time."

"I wanna go to the girls' night. Can I please go, Daddy?" Grace asked.

"Me too, Daddy. Please," Hope pleaded.

"No, it's for big girls." Hope's bottom lip started trembling while Grace pouted. "You're big girls; I meant to say adult girls. But you'll be with Grandma and Grandpa. Uncle Eden and I are going to a basketball game."

Hope crossed her arms and let out a frustrated sigh. Grace followed suit.

"What's the matter? You don't want to stay with Grandma and Grandpa?"

"I'm just joking, silly. We love Grandma." Hope laughed.

"And Grandpa. We love you, too, Grandpa," Grace added.

I shook my head, and everyone started to laugh.

My phone chimed, and I dug inside my pocket to pull it out.

> New, "You're obsessed with me. But it's cool. I miss you, too."

She attached a picture of herself with green gunk on her face and pink strips underneath her eyes.

> What's that?

> New, Peyton is giving me a facial. It's called selfcare.

> It looks painful.

> New, LOL. It's not at all. Maybe she'll give you one someday. It's her specialty."

> New, Well, anything girly is her specialty.

> I would be happy if Peyton would just say more than two-word sentences to me. If a painful face mask means I'm in there . . . I'll take it.

> New, LOL. Don't stress it. She'll come around.

> New, Send me a picture of what you're doing.

I took a picture of my plate of angel food cake and sent it to her.

> New, 😋 I'm so jealous. Save me a slice!"

> I got you.

> New, Gotta go. This thing is starting to burn.

> See! Painful.

I scrolled back up to her picture. Even with whatever that was on her face, she was beautiful. I laughed and put my phone back in my pocket.

"What's funny, Daddy?"

I looked up to find both my parents and my daughters staring at me.

I rubbed the back of my neck. "Nothing." I cleared my throat. "It was nothing, baby girl." I looked at my mom. "Mom, if there's any leftover, can I take an extra slice home?"

My mom gave me a warm smile. "Of course you can, baby."

***

I treated my brother to watch a basketball game that included one of his favorite teams. Growing up, our father taught us how to play basketball, and we both took a strong liking to it. Although I played on the varsity teams in both junior and senior high, basketball was just a hobby for me. For Eden, however, there was a time when it was his life. He received a scholarship to play at the collegiate level, but that was around the time when he started dabbling in the kind of drugs that couldn't be grown. He never played a game, and he ended up leaving school altogether.

That period of time was rough for my family, but I'm sure nothing compared to what he was experiencing. That was years before he and I made up and before he got clean.

We didn't reminisce on that time often, especially since much of it was a blur for him.

"Man, I can't thank you enough! And those seats? Nearly courtside. That was an amazing experience." Eden grinned.

"No doubt, bro. It was a good game. We need to do this with Dad next time. I'm sure he would really like that," I spouted.

"Yeah, he would. I've been thinking about that a lot more recently since finding out that we were expecting." Eden pulled at the knees of his jeans and straightened himself in the seat.

"What do you mean?" I prodded.

"Just Mom and Dad. They're getting older and slower. And while the past ten years of my life have been amazing, traveling and ministering alongside Daisha, meeting new people, being a part of God saving souls…" Eden looked out of the window for a brief moment and then back straight ahead. "I don't want to miss out on precious time, either."

I, of all people, knew how remorselessly short time could be.

"Ahh, so you're thinking of moving down here?"

"Yeah, man. Thinking about it, praying about it. I haven't spoken it over with Daisha yet, though. I know how much she enjoys our adventures together. Speaking of which, let me call her big head behind now and make sure she's good."

We laughed as he dialed his wife.

As they spoke, I selfishly thought about how much I would enjoy Eden and I to live in the same city. Our friendship started a few months after his last hospitalization. Soon after, he spent a little over a year in a rehabilitation facility, but I was still away finishing my undergraduate degree. By the time I finished my studies, he was in seminary school and getting married. Not long after that, they packed their bags to spend a year in Jerusalem.

We spoke often, and he visited as frequently as he could. He made sure to be here to celebrate my and Melissa's wedding, to congratulate us on the birth of our girls, and was here to ensure I made it through Melissa's funeral. Still, I wouldn't mind having him around for the smaller pieces of life, either.

"All right, Mamas. I love you." Eden beamed, ending his phone call.

"How is she?"

"Daisha? She's good…they sound like they're having a good time. But ask me what you're really trying to ask me." He chuckled.

"Man, whatever." I tried to laugh it off.

"Why don't you call her and check in, too?" Eden questioned.

I scratched the back of my neck. "New? Naw, man, she isn't like that. She doesn't need me. At least not in the way that I'm used to. Not in the way I expected." I cleared my throat, awaiting the speech that I was from Eden that would surely follow.

"Mm." He responded shortly, unlike himself.

I looked at him dumbfounded. "Is that it?"

"I have more I could say, but Daisha's been telling me that sometimes she just wants to vent. She doesn't want me to always have an answer."

I nodded my head. "I get that. But with me, I want the answers, man. Especially if you have one."

We shared a laugh.

"If you're comparing Zipporah to Melissa, you're going to get it wrong every single time, man. She might not need you in the same ways, but it doesn't mean she doesn't need you. It's likely just in a way you haven't figured out yet. Pay attention, you will."

I took a moment to chew on his words before responding. It wasn't something I was trying to do. It wasn't fair to her. To neither of them.

I found myself clinging desperately to my memories of

Mel, not wanting them to be drowned by my new emerging feelings for Z. I hadn't yet figured out a successful balance.

"But since you brought this all up…" Eden continued.

"Here we go," I interrupted.

Eden chortled and then continued, "Hey, man. You started it. But what's up with you and the whole new mommy thing with the girls?"

I ran my hand down my face. "Man…I really don't know. Since before I even reconnected with her, it's been new mommy this and that."

"If you get married again, wouldn't they technically have a new mother?"

I sighed. "I guess so." I drummed my fingers along the steering wheel and felt my chest tightening. "Mel couldn't wait to be a mom. When we found out we were having twins, I nearly passed out, but she was just overwhelmed with joy." I paused briefly, remembering that day and all the days thereafter, not realizing they were numbered. "She took all the classes and read every book. She sang to them from the day she found out. She wanted this. I know they don't remember her. I get that. I'm fully aware that they need someone to fill in the role she's no longer able to. But to let them call someone else Mom? I don't think I'm comfortable with that idea."

This time around, I took a page out of Daisha's book

and told Eden I would rather he not respond.

Shortly after moving to Atlanta, my parents suggested I visit a local church one of their friends had recommended. I had been visiting consistently for a few months and decided to make it home. I started helping out on a few different teams and decided to go to the earlier gathering on days I was serving.

I was sitting in the 8 a.m. service when I heard her. I looked up to find her singing on stage with the worship team. It could've been her or the stage lighting, but she glowed. Her voice was angelic, and still, couldn't hold a candle to her beauty.

After service, I found myself walking up to her. She was with her parents, and in front of them, I introduced myself and asked her out. She agreed.

Mel immediately took my breath away. I spent the next three years growing with and loving her. Unfortunately, I have spent more time mourning her and learning to live with her absence than I spent with her.

Even still, I often missed her, and I was sure I would always love her. If her death couldn't change that, nothing would.

Zipporah helped bring life to me in areas I presumed would be dead forever. I knew my heart was open to receiving both her and Peyton if they would have me. She was fire, and I desperately craved her warmth. I wanted to give her all the parts of me; she deserves nothing less. I just wanted to make sure that my love for her wouldn't erase all the things that Mel meant and brought to me. Especially in our children. *Wait, love?*

CHAPTER 11

"Then, we went to this Korean barbeque place, and it was so yummy. Dad had to make the meat; he almost gave me salmonella. But the food was still really good, Mommy. I could eat ramen every day, I think. We also went for a drive on his motorcycle, and before you ask, yes, I wore a helmet."

Peyton was singing the praises of her father. I was thrilled that she was having a good time getting to know her dad and making memories with him that I believed would last a lifetime.

"Mmm. Korean BBQ is so good. I miss the food in Los Angeles."

Atlanta was the reigning champ when it came to southern foods, but Los Angeles gave them a run for their money when it came to diverse cuisines.

"You should come and visit, Mommy. Maybe? It might be cool if we could all hang out...together."

"I don't think so, dude.... You know that," I started.

"C'mon, PeyPey. We have a long drive ahead of us. We need to get on the road," Eddie yelled from outside of her room door.

"Okay, Dad. I'm finishing up my call with Mommy, and then I have to show you my outfits," Peyton yelled back.

We were both pleasantly surprised when Eddie dedicated and decorated a room to Peyton instead of having her in a guest room. She was more than thrilled when he gave her his card to go shopping for clothes and furniture pieces to really make the room her own. I was happy that he was really throwing himself into this fully. I missed her ferociously, but if it meant she had two active parents, I was content with sharing.

"All right, Sweet P. Make sure to send me a million pictures of you with your grandparents and cousins. Tell your uncle I said hi, okay? I love you so much."

"Okay. And you send me pictures, too. Tell Nicole I miss her. I love you back very much." Peyton poked out her cheeks and made kissy noises which I returned. "Oh, and Mommy?"

"Yeah, babe?"

"Please, please switch the sweats for a skirt or the leather pants. The shiny ones." Peyton grinned from ear to ear in an attempt to persuade me.

I rolled my eyes playfully. "Bye, Peyton."

After hanging up with her, I decided to call Eddie to

check in on him.

"Hey, XYZ. What's up? Oh, and by the way, did you know it takes our daughter two to three hours to get dressed?"

I laughed. "Yup. She gets that from you, though. I hope you know that."

We reminisced on how Eddie would be in the bathroom for hours making sure his curls were always just right. This was also the same man who color-coded his sneaker collection. Yeah, she definitely got that from him.

"How are *you*, though? Have you spoken to Imani since she left?"

"No. She still isn't returning any of my calls." He puffed and we shared a moment of brief silence. "It's cool, though." He cleared his throat. "Peyton has been keeping me busy and distracted."

Before Eddie flew down to get Peyton, he let me know that Imani had broken up with him. He didn't get into much detail about it, and I didn't pry either. I didn't know much of her other than the fact that she was a twenty-two-year-old aspiring actress. I thought it was another one of his flings, but they surprisingly made it past his three-month mark and were together for a few years. I knew he had to be hurting. Eddie was a lot of things, but he wasn't impenetrable.

"I'm really sorry, Eddie," I consoled.

We spoke for a few more minutes until Peyton was finished modeling her third outfit option and decided on the first. I said a prayer for Eddie and headed off to brunch.

***

"Oooh. Hot momma alert." Nicole fanned herself dramatically. "You're smoking."

Nicole grabbed my hand and spun me around. I matched her energy and took powerful, modelesque strides, causing both Nicole and Daisha to erupt in a fit of laughter.

"From the West Coast, Peyton dressed me this morning."

I was already wearing a gray designer cropped sweatshirt and leather jacket when she called, but I decided to switch out my gray sweatpants for the patent leather pants like Peyton suggested. It did elevate and tie together the look, even though it felt like I would need to peel off the fabric later. She really did have an eye.

"You both look equally amazing. Let's take a picture together so I can send it to her."

We crowded around each other. Nicole held up the peace sign. Daisha pouted, giving us her best duck lip. And I smiled. A smile that radiated from my heart until it reached my eyes, making me squint a little.

Peyton immediately responded with three heart-eyes emojis.

> Favorite Daughter, You all look so pretty!

> "Thank you!"

> Favorite Daughter, I'm a little sour I'm missing out on this.

> Favorite Daughter, A lot sour.

> Favorite Daughter, But I'm also sooo happy for you, Mommy.

"Peyton approves. She says we all look so pretty."

"Awww, she's so sweet!" Daisha exclaimed.

"And apparently also a little sour."

They laughed, not fully aware of what I meant. I laughed, fully aware of the friendship that was blossoming right before me.

***

"Okay. I gotta hand it to you. This was spectacular, still…I'm not fully convinced I can give up meat forever."

Daisha had suggested we try a vegan restaurant for brunch. I had a sweet potato waffle, a plant-based scramble, and fried portobello mushrooms that honestly tasted like chicken.

"I know. It's not for everyone. I'm still trying to get Eden to come into the light, though. He eats meatless most days, but he won't commit, and I would love to raise our baby vegan...oops. Dang it!" Daisha mumbled.

"I knew it! Are you pregnant? Why didn't you tell me?" Nicole ranted as she pointed at Daisha like she was a traitor.

"I was trying to surprise you. We have an appointment in a few weeks where we'll get to figure out the gender. We want to do a reveal on Thanksgiving."

"Oooh, yes! I'm excited." Nicole clapped her hands together in elation.

"Congratulations, Daisha." I cheered.

Daisha looked over at me. "Thank you, friends! We're both excited. While we were never officially trying, we also weren't doing anything to prevent pregnancy, either. After a few years, I thought children of our own weren't in God's plans for us, and we were content with that. This was a sweet surprise."

Daisha nodded her head as if she was talking and hearing from God more than she was having a conversation with us. In the few hours I had known her, she spoke about her relationship with Jesus as if it was as palpable. She was only two years older than me, but she spoke and carried herself with such wisdom and grace. I desired deeply to have a relationship with God that was just as personal.

She was funny and appreciated my sarcasm and quick wit, which made us click instantly. Daisha had a deep ebony complexion and wore her jet-black curls in a top knot, showing off her tapered sides and high cheekbones.

Nicole offered to help with any details of the gender reveal, and I also extended my help. I looked over to Nicole, who was gushing with genuine love for both Daisha and her unborn child. She twirled her long wavy black hair in between her fingers as she asked questions that she swore would help her accurately guess the gender of the baby. Nicole was lively and full of moxie, but she also had the warmth of an old soul. She loved everyone she cared for unconditionally.

I thought briefly about my father and wished he was here to see me, and that all of his hopes and prayers for me were coming true. I came to a complete stop and forced my thoughts to stay on a happier track; my dad would've been happy for me. I can enjoy this. I don't always have to think of him and be swallowed whole by grief.

"You're coming to Thanksgiving dinner, right? You have to," Daisha asked, breaking my train of thought.

"Oh. I don't actually know. Zaire hasn't invited me… but I'm down to help you set up for the reveal either way."

Nicole shook her head. "Oh, he will. I know my brother.

He's in love with you."

"What?" I was so shocked I almost choked on air. "What do you mean? How do you know? No…no. He's not in love with me."

"If you say so. But I know what I know." Nicole shrugged her shoulders.

"No. You love love, Nicole. Every time it's your turn to pick a movie, it's a romance movie." I switched my eyes over to Daisha. "And not even light-hearted romantic comedy, I mean tear-jerking, love despite the cost, romance."

Daisha twisted her lips as she looked at me.

"What?" I asked.

"I don't know. Nicky is a hopeless romantic, but I wouldn't say she's wrong. I've heard portions of his conversations with Eden about you, and I don't even know if I would say he's fallen in love with you. I don't think he ever stopped."

I had never told anyone outside of my father and Peyton that I loved them. I never even said it to Eddie during our relationship. Granted, he never said it, either. I didn't have a meter for what romantic love would feel like outside of my imagination, books, and movies. The thought of experiencing that with Zaire gave me butterflies. *Wait, me? Butterflies?*

***

The knocking at my front door interrupted my thoughts, thankfully. I was seconds away from trashing the piece I had spent the last two weeks of my life molding and perfecting.

I skipped over to the door and unlocked it before opening.

"Hey, you."

He didn't respond but instead wrapped his arms around my lower back and lifted me off the floor. Once I was at eye level with him, he rested his forehead on mine. I watched as he closed his eyes and exhaled, and I decided to do the same. Everything about this man felt safe.

He made me feel so seen as I am. So understood. Respected. Admired. *Loved.*

"Hey, New. Okay." He placed me back on my feet after stepping through the doorway. "I really missed you, and I needed that. But now I'm ready for manual labor."

I turned around to hide my blush, led him into my small studio space, and flicked on the overhead lights.

"Okay, so this is the one I need help with." I pointed towards my latest work. The same woman in Virginia Beach who solicited me to paint my rendition of black boy joy now wanted a companion piece. This time of a black family in a backyard, however, on a much bigger canvas.

"I'm sure you would've made an incredible geneticist, but wow. You're a gifted artist."

Zaire walked around absorbing all of the hanging pieces and the finished sculptures.

"Thank you." I smiled proudly.

Zaire helped me wrap the finished work and package the box with cushion before carrying it to his trunk. While wrapping the piece in several protective layers, he asked me what my dreams were with art and if I had an end goal. I took a moment to think about it. I had done pretty well with selling pieces online. Most of my customers were people I met during my travels and their friends and family. I would love to be featured in an article where more people would have eyes on my work.

He walked back in after making a phone call. "Would you be okay with me changing our date plans tonight?" he asked, still looking at his phone.

"Yeah, sure. Is everything okay?"

"Yeah. We're still going out. Just not to the carnival anymore…and you're going to have to change." He looked at me now, smiling.

"I knew you were still afraid of heights!" I pointed an accusatory finger at him. "I wouldn't have forced you to get on any rides."

He gave a low chuckle. "You wouldn't have to. If you were getting on something, I would've forced myself. It's not that, though. I promise." He tucked his phone into his pocket. "But I am going to need you to wear a dress…and heels."

I folded my arms across my chest. "You sound like my daughter."

He laughed before kissing my cheek. "Just trust me. I'm going to drop off the painting for you, and I'll send you a picture of the tracking information. In the meantime, you get dressed."

***

"Wow, I don't know what to say…. I mean, of course, I'd be honored to!" I looked over to Zaire, grinning from ear to ear. He returned my look of excitement.

"Well, it's not a guaranteed spot. Your work would still need to be verified and selected by the board," Michelle Gao explained. "I make no promises, but I'm sure your work will speak for itself."

I nodded my head generously, trying to hide my smile. "No, absolutely. I understand…. The opportunity to submit and be considered alone is an honor. Thank you so much."

Michelle Gao gave me a tight smile and head nod before turning to Zaire and giving him a full smile and hug.

When I was sure she was out of earshot, I turned to Zaire and did a few small jumps, trying to keep my voice low. "How? How? How? How? That's Michelle Gao. *The Gao.*"

He smiled and grabbed my hand to help steady me in between jumps. "I didn't do much of anything. I just made a phone call."

"But how!"

Apparently, I was still a bit star-struck from meeting the woman who has single-handedly created some of the most well-known pieces in Asia and Europe and has recently been traveling the Western hemisphere to revitalize the art scene.

Zaire laughed before explaining that one of his previous students happened to be the nephew of Audrey Hampton, a well-known editor who has worked on different art publication magazines. He went on to say she said she owned him one and never thought it would be a favor he'd cash in on until tonight. Audrey made a few calls and was able to convince Michelle to offer me a slot in the "Creative And" contest, with next month's dedication to identifying new black and brown artists.

Overcome with emotion, I wrapped my arms around his neck and kissed him. His lips were stiff with shock at first and then softened to match my pace. His arms firmly and gently wrapped around my back.

Pulling away, "Um…" I cleared my throat. "I guess I should have just said thank you." I laughed and tried to search his face to see if I had overstepped any of his boundaries.

"This was so thoughtful…I just…"

This time, he stepped closer to me, closing off any space that might've still been in between us. He cupped my chin and lifted my face before kissing me this time, placing both hands on the small of my back, bringing all the fluttering feeling back to my stomach and all sorts of other feelings to the surface that I hadn't yet the words to name.

***

"You both can help me paint her hair. Just remember to go around the flowers."

"Okay, Ms. Z," Hope and Grace said in unison.

Together, we painted the mural on the bedroom wall I had been working on this past week while Peyton was away. It was a welcomed distraction because I wanted to FaceTime her every second of the day and needed to stop hovering.

"Breakfast is ready, girls!" Zaire called out from the kitchen.

We walked out of the bedroom, being sure to close the door behind us.

ALL THINGS BEAUTIFUL

"Thank you, Daddy," Hope said, raising both of her arms so that her father could lift her up and put her in the chair.

Grace followed, and he did the same with her before planting kisses on both of their cheeks.

"Thanks for making breakfast." I kissed him on the lips before taking my seat on the barstool.

The girls both giggled.

Together, we sat down, said grace, and ate our breakfast together as we had done every day this week.

Since our date, Saturday night, Zaire and I had been inseparable. While we both enjoyed our new closeness, it admittedly made respecting our boundaries a bit more difficult. We decided to have his girls around to help keep ourselves both busy and fully dressed.

"How's the mural coming along?" Zaire asked sneakingly while sipping his coffee.

I looked to both Hope and Grace. "How's it going, guys?"

They both lifted their fingers and acted like they were zipping their lips shut like we had practiced. While the girls knew what we were working on in their room, I wanted it to be a surprise to Zaire.

"Wow. You got my daughters to turn on me? My own

flesh and blood?" Zaire speculated.

    I nodded my head. "And it was easy, too. We're BFFs." I smiled at Hope and Grace, who both also nodded their heads.

    "Oh yeah?" Zaire planted his face in the palms of his hands and started making crying noises.

    I folded my arms over my chest, unbothered, but both girls hopped off their seats to comfort their dad.

    "It's okay, Daddy. Don't cry." Hope tried to rub his back but settled on his leg when she couldn't reach.

    Grace nodded. "I'm still your BFF, too, Daddy."

    "Are you sure?" Zaire fake whimpered. "Then, let's get her!" Zaire lifted his head and ran to pick me up before bringing me to the ground and tickling me.

    My laughs turned into snortling as Hope and Grace joined in.

    I was so happy with this man.

***

    "She looks so beautiful, Ms. Z." Grace held my hand and squeezed it.

    "She really is. You both look so much like her." I smiled.

Hope's lip trembled a bit. "You made our mommy so big."

"Mm-hmm. Do you like it, Hope?"

"I love it!" Hope exclaimed, pumping both hands in the air.

"Let's go get your dad now."

We went over to Zaire, who was on his laptop catching up on basketball stats. The girls made him cover his eyes, and he promised he wouldn't peek through his fingers. Once we were in the room together, the girls and I counted down from three. He removed his hands and stared at the almost larger-than-life mural on Hope and Grace's bedroom wall.

He asked me to paint something similar for the little girl I did while in Haiti. It was supposed to be a garden with flowers, birds, and butterflies. However, I added his late wife in the center of that garden. Her eyes were blue and in them, I added small stars and specs that Grace said looked like fairy dust. In her red, almost golden hair, I added sunflowers and vines. Melissa was a beautiful woman, and I hoped that this painting did her as much justice as she deserved.

While working on this together, the girls asked me so many questions about their mother that, of course, I couldn't or didn't know how to answer. I hoped that this would help them at least remember that, albeit short, she was here and that they both carried her with them.

"Do you like it? I know it's not exactly what we discussed, but it felt right. What do you think?" I asked Zaire, who hadn't yet said anything since opening his eyes.

He turned to me with tears in his now slightly reddened eyes. I tried to read his face, a mixture of appreciation and awe.

"I love you, Zipporah," Zaire professed, placing his hands over mine and holding them, anchoring himself as he turned to face me fully. "This means so much to me. *You* mean so much to me." He wrapped his arms around me, and for a moment, we stood silently, holding one another.

I was stunned. Inside of me were emotions swirling that I still couldn't put a name to, and yet, somehow, felt like they'd always been there. Was *this* love? Inside of me were doubts and insecurities rising to the surface. What would Peyton say? Would she be okay with this? Did he mean it? Did he really love me? What did that mean for my future? For our future?

I thought of my father, who often in my childhood would call me a daredevil. There wasn't a height or depth that I had ever backed away from. Like then, I decided to lean into this. Trusting that I would again land on both feet.

"I love you, too, Zaire. You mean just as much to me."

It was my first time saying it, but I meant it. And everything about saying it just felt right.

CHAPTER 12

"Do you think she's missed me just as much as I've missed her?" Zipporah looked at me, eager for my response, as if anyone who knew them would say otherwise.

I placed a hand on her shoulder in an attempt to soothe her. "I know she missed you just as much."

Peyton walked out of the terminal doors towards our car and nearly jumped in her mother's arms. They stood squeezing, holding, and swinging each other from side to side. I hauled Peyton's bags into the trunk of my car.

"It's good to have you back, Peyton. How was your trip?" I asked while holding both the front and back passenger car doors open.

"Thanks, Mr. Timothy. It was great." Peyton dismissed me quickly and looked back to her mom. "Actually, Mom…I have a small surprise…. *Please* don't be mad."

As if on cue, a tall, darker complexion man walked out of the same terminal and headed straight for my car.

"Peyton. Please explain yourself." Zipporah placed a hand on her hip and shifted her weight from one leg to the other.

"Dad was so sad, Mom. I mean *clinically* sad. I told him he could stay with us for a few days. Or in a hotel. He just needs us to help cheer him up," Peyton quickly added as her mother started to shake her head, prepared to say no.

"Hi, Eddie. It's good to see you," New said as she hugged her ex.

He picked her up and spun her. "XYZ! You haven't changed a bit. You look great." He set her down and looked her over fully, from head to toe.

"Thanks, Eddie," Zipporah laughed awkwardly, adjusting her shirt after he put her down. "This is my boyfriend, Zaire. Zaire, this is Peyton's father, Eddie."

I had never been confrontational in my life. Eden got into fights; I, on the other hand, usually talked him out of them. Nonetheless, everything about this encounter, including the way her ex kept eyeing her had me ready to go feral.

I shook off those thoughts and extended my hand. "Hey. Nice to meet you."

He shook it. "Good meeting you, too, man." He looked back and forth between New and me. "Hopefully, this isn't too awkward. I told Peyton I was more than open to visiting her, too, instead of her always flying to me. She insisted I fly back with her and stay a few days."

Zipporah crossed her arms. "Is that right?" She looked

over at Peyton. "Clinically sad, huh?"

I had a feeling Peyton was up to something.

***

"Thank you for picking them up at the last minute, Nicky. I owe you one," I spoke into the receiver.

"No worries! We're picking up some lunch and then heading to REACH. Do you need me to take them home with me? Or will you be able to pick them up?"

"I'll come by right after my last class. Thanks again, Nicky."

We exchanged goodbye and ended our call.

Austin came into my room earlier this morning and asked to speak with me during my free period. I didn't want to miss the opportunity to hear him out now that he was willing to talk to me.

I checked my time and said a prayer over Austin, myself, and the conversation we would have today. I asked the Holy Spirit to lead me in what I should say and prepare Austin's heart for whatever the Lord might be trying to say to him through me. As I said amen, a knock sounded at my slightly open door. I called out for Austin to come in and keep the door open.

"Hey, Mr. Timothy." Austin walked in with his head

low and his shoulders sunken. "Is now still good?"

"Yeah. Yeah, it is. You can have a seat anywhere you'd like."

He sat down in a chair near my desk, still not making direct eye contact. After a few minutes of him sitting there in silence, I decided to break the ice.

"How was your fall break? Did you do anything special?"

Still not looking up at me, he responded, "Not really. Just watched a shi…I mean, a lot of anime."

"Word? Personally, I've never gotten into anime, but I keep hearing about it. What would you recommend I start with?"

"Mmm." This time, he looked up at the ceiling, genuinely pondering an answer to my question. "I think you'd like *Dark Xena*. It's not too graphic, and the main background is a school. The villain in season one is actually the English teacher."

"Is that a spoiler?"

He chuckled. "No. Anime isn't like that. You find out who the villain is in the first ep."

"Okay, I'll check it out."

He nodded his head before going silent again.

I pulled up the show *Dark Xena* on my personal laptop and started watching. After the first gory scene, I decided it wasn't for me. But I was determined to make it through the first episode.

"Aren't you going to ask me questions?" Austin asked, interrupting the show.

I hit the spacebar to pause the episode. "Not if you don't want me to. We can just sit here. We can talk. I'm okay either way, as long as you are."

He shrugged his shoulders and dragged a chair next to my desk. I clicked on the spacebar again, restarting the show.

Twenty minutes into the show, Austin decided that he did, after all, want to talk. He shared with me that he started self-harming around the age of eleven. He said it happened accidentally at first; he was riding his bike and fell off a ramp and shattered his wrist. He said that while he felt pain, he also felt an intoxicating amount of release. Sometimes, he burned himself, but most often, he broke his hand or arm by either punching or throwing himself into walls.

When I asked about his parents, he said that his father was usually out of town for business and that his mother drank heavily when he was away. When they are together, it is usually intense from all of their fighting and bickering. He shared that they get along best when he's in a cast or in the hospital after hurting himself.

I did the first thing I could think to do, which was pray for him, but I knew he needed much more than that as well.

"Have you ever spoken to a counselor? Or seen a therapist? Either here at school or elsewhere?"

He leaned into his chair, obviously more relaxed. "Not really. I don't want my parents to get in trouble. And I especially don't want anything to happen to Jasmine. I'm supposed to protect her." He paused for a moment before smiling. "I do talk to Peyton. She's easy to talk to."

Oh boy.

"My older brother Eden is actually a licensed social worker and counselor. You can't tell me something like this and expect me not to point you in the direction of someone who could better help. It's not that I'm not here for you. I just think it'll also be beneficial if you talk to someone who has been where you are and has the proper training and tools."

"I'd rather not do that." Austin kicked his feet off the second chair he'd propped them on. "You said I could trust you. You said you helped another kid before at your old school."

"That's because you can trust me, Austin. And while I did, I have to be honest with you: his situation wasn't this. Think about it this way. What if it was Peyton? What if Peyton came to you and told you she was hurting herself, and you knew someone who could help her through this?

What would you do?"

He sat back down in the chair and decided to hear me out. I shared some of Eden's story with him and what it was like growing up being constantly worried about him not waking up from his high. He explained he didn't want Jasmine worried about him in those same ways and decided he would talk to him.

We clapped hands as the bell rang, signaling the end of his study hall and the end of my free period. He thanked me for listening. I thanked him for being open with me.

Like my former student Bryson, I was determined to do what I could to help see him through.

***

"I've missed you." New embraced me and laid her head on my chest.

I buried my face in her mess of curls and inhaled my favorite scent. "I've missed you, too."

It had only been a few days since we'd seen each other, but I missed her deeply. I missed her laugh echoing off the walls of my home. I missed seeing her sneakers sprawled out by the front door. I missed making breakfast with her and watching her connect with my girls. I even missed her forcing me to watch replays of old Marvel and DC TV shows.

I needed her.

I thought it would take time for me to get used to her, time for her to fill up all the space I was making for her, but it happened easily. And I allowed it to. Zipporah had made it clear to me, without me ever asking it of her, that she understood what Melissa meant to me. What I wanted her to mean to my daughters. She found her own way to let me know she, too, could make room.

With the end of fall break, we both went back to our typical work schedules. She had also been at meetings and on calls during the day since being accepted for the "Creative And" expo and publication. Not to mention, with her ex Eddie in town, Peyton wanted to do things with both of her parents. I got it; she had never experienced eating with them, watching movies with them, or doing mundane household activities with both of them. Still, I couldn't help but feel excluded. I wanted to create a relationship with Peyton but hadn't yet figured out an entry point, if one for me even existed.

Today, Zipporah invited me to go bowling with them.

Peyton cleared her throat, breaking my embrace with her mother. "Dad, you remember my English teacher, Mr. Timothy, right?" Peyton quickly looked at me and then faced her father.

"Yes, I do. This is the boyfriend." Eddie got up and clapped hands with me. "Wow, XYZ, You actually have a boyfriend. We lived together for almost two years, and I don't think you've ever called me boyfriend." He tipped his hat towards me. "Must mean he's one of the good ones."

Zipporah leaned into my shoulder. "He is." She smiled. "You're not so bad yourself, Eddie. Don't forget that."

We did two full rounds of bowling with Eddie and me both neck and neck. While Zipporah was extremely competitive and halfway mad at me for winning, she couldn't bowl to save her life. In between rounds, Eddie and I spoke friendly about a little of everything. We didn't have much in common, but he was genuine and that made him okay with me. The way he and Zipporah laughed and teased each other to onlookers may have looked flirty, but up close, it was nice. They carried the same kind of banter I did with both Daisha and Nicole. Above all, I could respect a guy who wanted to do right by his daughter.

"Seems like you won again, man," Eddie spoke, breaking me away from my thoughts.

"You can beat him, Dad!" Peyton cheered.

I made sure to hold a straight face, but that stung a little.

"Nope, PeyPey. I'm going to sit it out. He's won fair and square."

Zipporah slid into the booth next to me, and Eddie slid in next to Peyton, who sat across from me.

"Fine." She snickered, rolling her eyes at me.

Okay, now that was intentional.

"I saw that, PeyPey," Eddie retorted.

"What? What did I miss?" Zipporah asked.

"Nothing, Mommy. I'm sorry, Mr. Timothy." Peyton looked at me, holding a plastered smile.

"What's going on, Sweet P? We can go outside and talk in private?" Zipporah reached over the table and held her daughter's hand.

Peyton shook her head no, now looking down at her lap.

As much as I loved Zipporah and didn't want to go back to a space that existed without her, I couldn't allow myself to be the thing causing strife in their relationship.

"I'm sorry, Peyton. If things with me and your mom are making you uncomfortable, you can say that, and I'll respect it."

Zipporah looked at me and gulped. I could tell she didn't want to hear that as much as I didn't want to say it.

Eddie held up his hands. "Hey, PeyPey. I think I might've said something on one of our calls that made you feel this way."

"No, Dad. You didn't do anything wrong," Peyton

declared.

"Yeah, but that's because no one did. I told you I love your mom, and that's because I do." He looked at Zipporah and smiled. "Your mom's the coolest. You know that. But we're friends. We've always worked best as friends."

"And I love your dad," Zipporah expressed. "He was a great friend to me while I was going through a really rough time. We're family. We'll always be family thanks to you, Sweet P. But we're not getting back together. We've never really been together…not like that." Eddie laughed, and then Zipporah laughed.

I decided to get out of the booth and allow them to have this time alone.

I slid my phone out of my pocket once outside and noticed I had a dozen missed calls from my mom, Daisha, and Nicole. Frantically, I called my mother back, who answered on the first ring.

"Hey, Mom. Are you okay? What's going on?"

"Baby…" She paused. "Are you alone?"

"No, Mom. I'm out with Zipporah and Peyton. What is it? Mom, talk to me."

"Have Zipporah drive you to the hospital."

"The hospital? What's going on, Mom?" My mind quickly thought of Daisha and her baby, then Eden, who

I knew had been sober for the last fifteen years. Lastly, I thought of my father, and something quickened in me the more I thought of him. "What's wrong with Dad, Mom?"

I heard my mother start to sniffle, and that eventually led to her crying. I couldn't stand to hear my mother crying.

I heard in the background Nicole asking for the phone.

"Hey, Nicky. Just tell me, man." My voice started to crack.

"It's your dad, Z. He's in the hospital."

CHAPTER 13

A week had gone by.

One whole week.

I thought when I offered to drive Zaire to the hospital, I was being considerate. He shouldn't have had to drive while he was worried about his dad. I thought when I offered to hold his hand as we walked down the hall I was being kind. I thought that when I decided to go into the hospital room with him when we arrived, I was being strong for him. But I wasn't. I couldn't be.

Everything about being in the hospital room brought back terrorizing memories I thought I had buried years ago. But with every beep of a machine, more and more of the calm I was clawing onto for dear life left. The final straw was when he said my name and smiled at me. The same way my dad did years ago before he closed his eyes for a final time.

All at once, my dad was dying over and over again in my head. As if he could sense something in me was breaking, Zaire looked at me and asked if I was okay. But I wasn't. I couldn't be.

So, I left.

ALL THINGS BEAUTIFUL

I couldn't take it. I couldn't breathe. I just couldn't.

"Mommy, Dad's taking me to school, okay? I'm riding back with Nicole after REACH."

I pulled the covers off me to kiss Peyton before she left. "Okay, Sweet P. Have a great day." I kissed her cheek, and she kissed mine back.

"Mommy." Peyton palmed the sides of my face. "Will you please eat something today?"

"I will try. I promise."

Peyton left my room and closed the door behind her. While every bone in my body longed to go back to bed, I needed to shower. I needed to do something other than lie down and feel my soul literally slipping further and further into a darkened pit of sadness.

This time, I couldn't control it. I couldn't will myself to feel something else. I couldn't distract myself. I just couldn't.

I stood in the shower until my skin pruned. It took so much energy to wash my body and brush my teeth. I finally lugged my body out of the shower and lotioned up. My hair needed to be washed and detangled, but I was already feeling exhausted and decided to deal with it another day. I threw on an old, tattered tee shirt and a pair of shorts. Although both items were purchased to be oversized, I noticed how loose the material was around me. I spent most of my days in bed and had to force myself to eat, and these days, that consisted of downing enough water to stay hydrated.

I walked over to the kitchen and noticed everything was in pristine condition. Peyton and I weren't messy people but it didn't even look lived in. I opened the door of the refrigerator and found an assortment of foods packed in Tupperware containers. The biggest one with a sticky note attached.

> Hey girlfriend,
>
> I made all of your faves.
>
> Love,
>
> Your favorite next-door neighbor/friend/sister, Nicole.

I opened the containers to find lasagna, a kale Caesar salad, chicken bowls with rice and beans, and a big container of banana pudding.

My head sank in shame. *Her* family was in the hospital, and here she was, taking care of *me*. I didn't deserve her. I didn't deserve any of them.

I didn't eat. I didn't even try. I couldn't.

***

Incessant knocking on the front door woke me up from a dream. Well, a nightmare. The same one I've been having all week. I'm at the hospital, the one where my dad passed, only he isn't there.

I pleaded with my body to get up from the bed beneath me and open the door. It finally responds, and my feet hit the floor. Through the glass, I'm greeted by a familiar toothy grin and reluctantly open the door.

"Hey, Eddie. Peyton told me you were leaving today." I briefly gave him a hug and plopped my body on the couch.

He sat on the loveseat facing me. "I was, but it didn't sit right with me leaving just yet. I have my assistant shipping me my laptop so I can work from here for the time being."

I wiped my face with the back of my hand. "You don't have to do that, Eddie. I wouldn't want anything happening at your job while you're away."

Eddie shrugged. "My team's got it. I pay them enough to be able to step away for a few weeks. Besides, you're family, XYZ. I'm here for you if you'll let me be. Besides, if Peyton keeps feeding me the way she has been, I may just move down here."

"Peyton doesn't cook. The food is from my neighbor."

"Oh. Well, whoever they are, let them know they have a fan."

For the first time today, I laughed.

I peered up at Eddie and blinked away my tears until he came into focus. He had smooth, rich skin and stood tall at six-foot-two. His head, full of short, lush curls, now had strands of gray peppered in them, only adding to his charm. The man was handsome, no doubt about it.

I thought back to the younger version of him I met at a party. We spent the night not talking about much of anything, and I appreciated his silent company. We ended the night entangled, to say the least. He radiated a lightness that I wanted to experience desperately back then. We ended up being really good friends who kept trying to make something more out of our relationship. A few months after Peyton was born, we decided we liked each other better when we weren't together together.

While Peyton invited him to stay with us on her very own *Parent Trap*, I'm glad she did. It gave us time to remember we still enjoyed each other's company and really got a kick out of making each other laugh.

I nodded. "Thanks for being here, Eddie."

"Don't mention it. I'm about to order some takeout. Do you want anything?" Eddie asked, scrolling on his phone.

"No, thanks. I do have enough food in the fridge to feed a family of five. Help yourself."

Eddie wasted no time and propelled himself from my

living room to the kitchen in a flash. He fixed himself a little of everything and warmed up his plate. I watched him eat, not because I was hungry, but more so because I was starting to feel worried at the continued absence of my hunger.

"Wait, is the person who made you the lasagna the same person who made this banana pudding?" Eddie asked, inhaling another spoonful of the desert. "Is this all that same neighbor?"

"Yup. Nicole, my next-door neighbor…and friend."

Saying her name out loud made me feel even more embarrassed for how many of her calls and texts I had ignored over the past week. Nicole had become more than just a friend to me.

Sister.

I thought back to the note she left. Friend was an understatement. She was my sister.

I knew I could talk to her. I wanted to talk to her. I just…couldn't.

And for the fifth time today, I buried my head inside of my tee shirt and cried.

I couldn't make out whatever words Eddie was saying over the sound of my own intrusive thoughts.

I am hungry. I'm unraveling again. I won't make it out

this time. I don't deserve them. I am hungry. I'm a bad friend. I'm a horrible girlfriend. I don't deserve to be a part of this family. I am really hungry. I can't even mother my own child properly. I'm drowning in this darkness, and there isn't anyone who could save me. If my dad could see me, he would be so disappointed in how I turned out. I'm a waste. And I'm hungry.

With the strength I could muster up, I carried myself to bed and wrapped my body in the sheets. I should return Nicole's call. I need to be strong for Peyton. I want to be present for Zaire. But I just couldn't.

CHAPTER 14

I knew it the moment I felt her hand trembling in mine that she wasn't okay.

I went over to my mom and dad and spoke to them briefly. By the time I turned around to check on her, she was gone. Again, like before, she was gone.

The shuffling of my first-period students into the classroom grabbed me out of my train of thought. I greeted my class and began walking around handing out a week's worth of graded papers, quizzes, and other assignments. The past week had me out of my routine and slightly behind on my schedule.

As I passed Peyton several of her A+ assignments, I couldn't help but wonder how her mom was really doing.

"Hey, Peyton, would you mind stepping to my desk for a moment?"

Peyton nodded, not looking at me while getting out of her desk.

I sat in my chair and waited until she approached.

"Hey…um." I cleared my throat nervously and whispered, "How are you? And um…how are things?"

Peyton nervously started to fiddle with a beaded bracelet on her wrist. She chewed the corner of her lip, and she twisted around the material, reminding me of her mother. I was worried about Zipporah, but now I was also concerned about how this all might be affecting Peyton.

"Are you asking about my mom?" Peyton answered in a whisper.

"Well, no. Yes, but…um. I also want to know how you're doing, considering."

"Can we talk during lunch?"

I nodded my head. "Sure. That works."

***

"I'm glad you're feeling so much better, Dad. Glory to God."

"Glory to God." My dad shook his head in agreement.

"All right, Dad. I'm going to let you get some rest now. I'll be in to check on you and Mom after Daisha and I have lunch." I watched the screen as Eden got his phone from my father and hugged him.

"You don't have to keep checking in on me. I'm okay. Healthier than most my age, the doctor says. And that goes for both of you." My dad looked at the screen towards me.

"We're always going to check on you and Mom.

Especially now, old man," I confirmed.

"Joyce, do you hear your son calling me old?" my dad called out.

"Don't put me in it, Robert." My mom laughed.

We shared a laugh together before ending our phone call.

My mom shared with us that my dad had been complaining of headaches. She pleaded with him to go get it checked, but he declined. When the headache would not wear off with Tylenol, and he started to feel an uneasy tightening in his chest, he relented and decided to go get checked out. Thankfully, he did not have a heart attack or stroke, but the doctors did find his blood pressure was elevated, as were his cholesterol levels. The doctors prescribed him a few medications and suggested a change in his diet, one he wasn't fond of but agreed to.

I thought that sharing the news with Z would help her feel better, but it had been one week and she still wasn't answering any of my texts or calls.

"Hey, Mr. Timothy." Peyton strolled into the classroom and sat in the chair she typically sits in near the front during class.

"Hey, Peyton. Thanks for agreeing to talk with me."

"Yeah…no problem."

I ran a few questions in my mind, trying to discern what would be the best way to have this conversation and exactly what conversation I was trying to have.

"Austin says he eats his lunch here, and he spends most of his study halls here with you. He says he likes talking to you. Talk to me like how to talk to him," Peyton asserted.

In the past few weeks following fall break, Austin and I had spent more and more time talking with one another and watching his favorite anime. I noticed how often he mentioned Peyton. How she was easy to talk to. How she prefers to wear her hair straight even though it's pretty curly. How she always found a way to make her uniform unique and colorful. He definitely had a thing for her, whether he realized it yet or not. I was just happy that he was speaking to someone licensed and working through his issues with someone who could really help.

"Okay. I do want to know how your mom is doing. I haven't heard from her since last week, and I'm worried. I also want to know how you're doing. You seem nervous and not like yourself."

Peyton folded her arms defensively across her chest, looking more and more like her mother. "You think you know me?"

"No. I'm not saying that. I would like to, though. I don't see a reality I'm comfortable with where things with Zipporah go the way I hope without us having some sort of relationship."

Peyton opened and closed her mouth a few times, I assume not sure how to respond.

"I consider myself to be a patient man, though," I continued. "I'm okay with earning your trust and respect. Maybe that can start here with you being honest and telling me how you're doing."

"I don't know. I'm okay, I guess. But my mom…. She's not okay. I've never seen her like this before. She's sad and crying all the time. She's not working with Nicole at REACH and I don't even think she's working on her pieces for the publication thing she told me about."

Peyton stopped for a moment, reached inside her glittery pink book bag, and retrieved her iPad. "I did some research online and found a report from the American Journal of Psychiatry; it's about complicated grief. I know my mom doesn't like when I diagnose her but some of the things in here sound familiar. Especially the parts about not being able to function in your daily routine." Peyton paused again, almost as if she was considering sharing or not.

I motioned for her to continue.

"She hasn't been eating. She hasn't been doing anything. She just looks tired and cries all the time."

My heart started beating on the outside of my chest. I was determined. I was seeing her today, not calling or texting, but showing up at her home. I had to be there for her.

"I'm sorry, Mr. Timothy…"

Surprised was an understatement.

Peyton continued, "I've been more than just mean to you. And I'm sorry."

I scratched the back of my neck. "It's all right. I guess I can understand you feeling a way about my relationship with your mother when I'm your teacher."

"Yeah…. I can't lie; that's weird." She laughed and then folded her legs underneath her. "But when I was doing my research, I found something that said you can mourn and grieve for people who aren't gone."

I leaned back in my chair, interested in what she had to say. "What do you mean?"

"Well…. It's just that…. I've never seen my mom with a guy before. Like ever. And I could tell that she really liked you. I guess that just made me feel like the more she got closer to you, the more our relationship would change."

"That's profound. I knew you were an astute student, but you're really into this psychotherapy thing."

She smiled. "Yeah. A fashionable one. You have to remember that part."

I laughed. "I will. But you know…some things will change, sure. If your mom and I get married, that will mean we'd probably all live together. And that would be an adjustment. But one of the things I respect about you and your mom is the unique relationship you guys have together. You guys are friends, and I don't want to get in the way of that ever." I considered my words in my own situation. "If I'm being honest with you…I've been really concerned with how my relationship with your mom would change the one I have…or had with my late wife. I kept trying to hold onto things, not wanting them to change. Not wanting to feel like I've changed. And I guess the truth is that I have. Things will inevitably change, but it doesn't need to be all bad, though."

"Hmmm. Can I use that last part for my practice?" Peyton asked, sounding more like her usual peppery self.

I laughed again and nodded. "Go ahead. You're good at this."

"Thanks…" Peyton got up and started to rearrange her book bag. "So, you're going to marry my mom?"

"I'd like to. I haven't told anyone that, but yes. I don't have a ring or anything yet, so don't tell her. I would like her to be my wife and for us all to be family. How do you feel about that?"

She shrugged. "I'm not sure yet. But I do have a few conditions."

"Hit me."

"Friday nights are our movie nights. H & G can come… sometimes. But no boys allowed."

"Okay, is that all?"

"I'm guessing me sleeping in her bed is out?"

I chuckled. Zipporah had shared with me that oftentimes, Peyton would fall asleep or wake up in the middle of the night to go to her bed. And while my girls made a habit of sneaking into mine early every morning, I had plans of my own for our marital bed.

"Probably for the best," I answered.

"Eww. Don't be gross." Peyton scrunched up her face.

I chuckled again, this time harder.

As she walked out of my classroom, I silently prayed that this was just the beginning of whatever our relationship would grow into, at whatever pace she was comfortable with.

***

When she opened her front door, I almost didn't recognize her. Her hair wasn't in the typical lush of curls she put in a bun or wore down framing her face, but a matted tangled mess. Her eyes, which usually shone through those honey-colored orbs, were now dimmed, swollen, and red.

She also seemed a bit thin.

"Zaire, please…"

I didn't care to hear her protest. I picked her up and carried her to the living room. Once she was seated, her protesting continued, but I reached inside the grocery store bag and pulled out the bowl of soup I purchased along with crackers, Gatorade, and a piece of chocolate cake because if it was one thing she couldn't resist, it was sweets.

"Zaire, please. You're not listening. I don't want you to be here right now. I need more time."

I looked at Zipporah and wondered if she knew how much time away from her had torn me apart before. I wasn't letting that happen again.

"I can't leave."

She lifted the inside hem of her tear shirt and wiped her eyes. "I need you to go, though. Please. I don't want you to see me this way."

"I don't care about any of that. I can't leave you." I twisted off the cap on her drink and removed the lid off the soup. "Now, please, let me feed you."

"Why?"

"Because it doesn't look like you've been feeding yourself."

ALL THINGS BEAUTIFUL

"No. Why won't you leave?"

I put the spoonful of soup down and faced her. She clearly had no idea what she meant to me.

"I love you. I loved you when we met in Aspen on the ski lift. I loved you until I saw you again on the Ferris wheel in Myrtle Beach. And there, I loved you more. I've loved you every day since I knew you, and I can't leave because I can't risk not seeing you, not hearing you, not being with you for another fifteen years. I can't."

She buried her face into the palms of her hands and cried a cry eerily reminiscent of her scream the last time I saw her in the hospital with her father.

I wrapped my arms around her and held her. I didn't understand what was going on with her. I had never heard the term complicated grief before. Maybe I experienced that when Mel died unexpectedly, but I'm unsure. I was surrounded by family who were more than ready to help me in any way that I needed. And more than that, I had the love of my father, who never once wavered, even while I was upset with him. He carried me through when I couldn't find the strength to do so for myself.

"If I could carry the weight of this for you, I would. I would kill myself trying to. But there's someone who can, and He could do it so much better than me. I love you so much, and I'm not leaving you. But He loves you so much more than I will ever be able to. His love is perfect, and it's available to you if you let Him."

I sat and rocked her as she cried. I prayed over her and with her when she was ready to pray. I fed her when she admitted she was hungry. I washed and combed her hair, hoping she would see that I could take care of her if she let me. When she finally stopped crying and fell asleep, I made myself comfortable on the couch, just in case she needed me during the night. Because I wasn't leaving.

CHAPTER 15

"Mommy! Did you hear me?" Peyton asked, tapping my shoulder.

I removed an earbud out of my ear, stopping the music. "Sorry, Sweet P. I didn't hear you come in." I bent at the waist and kissed her cheek. "What did you say?"

"Can I go to Paige's house? Jasmine and I want to go help her. She thinks she may have gotten her period. Her mom will be at work until midnight, and she's freaking out."

"Okay. Her mom's a nurse so I'm sure she has got it covered, but you can go and help her nerves. Where's your dad?"

"Thanks, Mommy. And he's in my room."

"Is he on a call?" I asked since he hadn't come into the room to say hello.

"Yeah. He's been at this same meeting since he picked me up."

"They're probably losing it since he's been gone so long."

ALL THINGS BEAUTIFUL

Eddie had made do with his promise to be here. I didn't expect to be able to count on him, but I was glad to stand corrected. He made himself available to pick up and drop Peyton off at school to make sure I didn't have to miss any counseling appointments and my fluctuating schedule with the "Creative And" edit.

Audrey Hampton was extremely understanding of my situation when I asked to back out for the winter edition. Zaire was also understanding but mentioned it might be therapeutic for me to put my feelings into my work. I spoke with my counselor about it, and she neither encouraged nor discouraged me but left space for me to make a decision that felt best. I found myself spending most nights awake in the studio. While I tried to do everything, it did feel natural to pick up a brush. One thing led to another, and I decided to continue working on my collection for the edit.

"Yeah…maybe. You think he'll go back soon?" Peyton asked in a slightly somber tone.

I turned away from my canvas to give Peyton my full attention. "He probably will, dude. But he's always going to be your dad, even in California. You have your own room there, much bigger than your room here, and you can visit him anytime you'd like."

"I guess so. I'm just going to miss him, Mommy. It won't be the same. He'll go back to work, and he'll forget about me." Peyton started to chew on her trembling lip.

I went to console her and rocked her in my arms, kissing the top of her head.

"You are unforgettable, Pey," Eddie's voice croaked, startling both of us.

Peyton left my arms and went and hugged her father. He looked at me, twisting his lip. In the past few weeks since he'd been here, I'd gotten to see first hand Eddie and Peyton form a bond of their own. While it was comforting to watch them grow to both know and like each other, our current living situation was less than ideal.

Eddie was spending his nights in Peyton's bedroom, which meant Peyton was sleeping in mine. Eddie's assistant shipped him three computers, a laptop, and a monitor, which were all currently set up in my living room. And the collective I was currently working on was expanding past the small confines of my makeshift studio. Not to mention when Zaire came over with his girls. The small condo I purchased when we moved here, with plans for us to grow into, was proving to be far too quaint the more our lives expanded with people.

Thinking of all the people in our lives reminded me that Nicole and Daisha would be coming over for a girls' night shortly. I hadn't spent much time with either of them the past three weeks while I was working on pulling myself together. Nonetheless, Nicole managed to drop meals off every other day on her way to REACH, and Daisha called me every morning to pray with me. I really hit the friendship jackpot.

***

There was a knock at my door once, then a pause, and then the knock resumed three more times before pausing and ending with two final knocks. I didn't even need to check. I knew it was Nicole.

I unlocked the front door and met my smiling friend.

"Hey, girlfriend," Nicole sang.

I laughed. "Hey, girlfriend. It's been so long I actually missed you."

"Me?" Nicole fanned herself dramatically. "You missed me? Wooow."

We laughed and hugged each other.

"Okay, Eddie," I called out from the kitchen. "My friend is here. Time for you to go."

Eddie walked out of Peyton's room, still looking down at his phone. He had been in back-to-back meetings and calls. I hoped everything was really okay with him having been away from work for so long.

"Okay, okay. I'm leaving. And to think I thought we were friends." Eddie stuffed his phone back into his pocket and lifted his head, staring at Nicole.

I looked at Nicole, who was also staring back at Eddie.

"Oh! I'm sorry. You guys haven't met." I stood in between the two. "Eddie, this is my really good friend, Nicole. Nicole, this is Eddie. Peyton's father."

Eddie stuck on his hand and held it open. "Are you the friend married to Zaire's brother?"

Nicole reached out her hand and shook his. "Nope, that's Daisha. I'm the other friend and neighbor."

Eddie's face grew up into a smile as he continued to hold onto her hand. "No way you're the neighbor cooking up food like a forty-five-year-old aunty. Those ribs put me to sleep like a baby."

Nicole blushed. "That's me. Cooking is my passion. Well, my second or third passion. I don't know. It's somewhere in the mix with dancing and being a real-life aunty."

Eddie laughed, still holding her hand.

The doorbell rang, indicating someone else was now at the door. I walked backward to the door, still watching the coquettish exchange happening between Eddie and Nicole.

I unlocked the door and allowed Daisha to come in. Although she didn't look it, I felt her growing bump as we hugged.

"Hey, girl! You look good." Daisha rejoiced.

"Thank you, friend. As do you! How are you? How's baby?"

"We're both good." Daisha ran a hand over her now visible bump before peering over my shoulder to register the faces of the people within earshot.

I turned around and welcomed her into my home.

"Hey, Daisha, this is Eddie, Peyton's father. Who is leaving, by the way," I stressed. "And Eddie, this is Daisha."

They smiled politely at one another, and I made a mental note of how quickly Eddie's attention went back to Nicole.

I cleared my throat, reminding him it was time to leave.

Eddie saluted me with two fingers to his forehead, grabbed his jacket, and left.

As if Nicole snapped out of her trance, she looked at both Daisha and me and smiled, "Okay. We have so much to cover. Who wants to go first?"

***

I used the back of my hand to dry my eyes, and Daisha rubbed small circles on my upper back.

"I didn't even know that was a thing, you know? It was difficult and even embarrassing trying to explain exactly how I was feeling and all the thoughts whirling inside of my head. I'm so glad I found her. She has been quite literally a lifesaver. And joining the grief group at church has been equally amazing. They just get it."

Nicole leaned towards me and grabbed my hands. "I'm so happy. You look and sound so much better. I'm really happy for you."

I smiled and gave her hands a small squeeze.

"Thank you. And thank you for being cool with taking some time away from REACH the past few weeks. I needed it, and now I'm ready to come back."

Nicole clapped and then tried to settle her excitement. "Are you sure? I mean, we are kind of bursting at the seams, so many more kiddos are registered and scheduled to start in the new year. But still, we can hold it down if you need more time."

I shook my head excessively, "Nope. I want to come back. The pieces I was working on for the collective are all just about finished. And I need to get out of here during the day. Not sure how much longer I can take hearing Eddie babble on about gaming programs and drops during the day."

Nicole nodded, smiling.

"So, what's next? How can we support you while you're healing?" Daisha asked.

"You guys are supporting me so much just by being

here. You both have no idea. When my dad died, I spent so much of that time alone. Sure, I eventually saw a counselor, but the second I stopped feeling completely depressed and empty, I went back to school. I kept myself and my mind busy. Yeah, there was Eddie, but he's not the same person now. Back then, we were both kids, and I had no idea how to express myself, let alone rationalize how I was feeling and what I needed. Before I knew it, I had Peyton, and I just kept keeping myself busy. Never *really* healing because I didn't know I needed to." I sighed, thinking about how so much of my life has changed in the past three months. "But now I have you guys. And Peyton, who, by the way, claims she correctly diagnosed me first." I let out a laugh. "Even Eddie has been reliable and just here. And Zaire…Zaire is…everything."

"Awwww! You love him?" Nicole asked in full-blown excitement.

I nodded my head. "I do. I really do." I waved my hands in the air as if dispersing the feelings. "Okay, okay. Enough of my stuff. What's been up with you, Nicole?"

She threaded a chunk of her hair with her fingers and curled the final strand around her index. "Mmm…nothing much. Besides what's been happening with REACH, honestly, nothing new."

"How was the date with that one guy with the mustache?" Daisha asked.

"Oh yes! You did say you had a date with him." I turned to face her fully, recalling the guy she said approached her at the grocery store.

"I forget about him." She giggled. "The date was nice. We went to dinner. And he was nice, don't get me wrong… there just wasn't a spark."

"Ahh, that is a bummer. You, of all people, definitely deserve that spark," Daisha confirmed.

"Was there a spark with Eddie?"

Both Nicole and Daisha's heads snapped in my direction.

I raised my hands. "I'm not blind. You both were staring each other down, and there was a vibe. I'm just saying."

Nicole smiled. "I don't know. I just met him, and I was being nice."

"Be so serious, Nicky," Daisha protested.

"I am being serious. I think he's very handsome, but that's all." Nicole pouted and cocked her head. "Is that weird for me to say? With him being Peyton's dad and all?"

"No, not at all." I confessed, "Eddie and I have always worked better as friends. Honestly. Nothing romantic, no lingering feelings, just friends. And I know for a fact you're his type."

ALL THINGS BEAUTIFUL

Daisha burst out in laughter, and Nicole pushed me.

In between laughs, I managed to say, "The way he all but froze looking at you? You're definitely his type."

Nicole tried to hide her blush by dismissing me. "What about you, Daisha? What's new with you?"

I obliged her and shifted in my seat towards Daisha.

"I'm good. I'm so happy. Besides when I'm tired and annoyed with Eden." She laughed. "But we're both so happy. Baby is measuring at fourteen weeks, and our due date is April 30th. Eden and I have decided to settle here."

Nicole squealed. "Yay! I'm so happy to have you both here."

"That's really exciting," I added. "What was the determining factor for you both?"

"Mmm. Honestly, we both just felt it was time. I brought it up just to see how he felt about it, but to my surprise, he was already feeling the same way."

The night went on with us splitting pizza, singing karaoke, and sharing stories. Nicole shared her very long and detailed list of the qualities that she believed made a perfect husband. I couldn't help but compare her list to Eddie, and was surprised that while he didn't carry all of the traits, he carried the ones that mattered. Daisha expressed her excitement about looking for a home, explaining that they'd never purchased property together since, with all of their traveling, they never needed to.

To my surprise, I openly shared stories and pictures of my dad without shedding any tears. My therapist encouraged me to lean into the people in my life and believe that they would be both willing and able to support me. I was overjoyed to be experiencing that they were indeed, solid.

***

"Are you ready?"

I looked up from my fidgeting hands into Zaire's hazel eyes. How his stare was both delicate and intense was beyond me. He reached over and rested his hand on the side of my face.

"You're not doing this alone; I'm right here with you," he affirmed.

I smiled and kissed the inside of his palm. "Okay, I'm ready. Let's go."

Both my counselor and grief group advisor recommended that I do something to help me come to terms with the loss of my father in a healthy way. I had never visited the grave site of my dad, not since I watched them lower him into the ground years ago. While other members of the group visited a location where they shared a memory with the person they lost, I decided I would come back here to the place where I lost a part of myself, along with my father.

With Zaire's fingers intertwined with mine, I led the way to my father's. I continued walking until both of my feet were planted inches away from my father's tombstone. I let out a staggering breath as I touched the gray engraving.

Jeremy Smith. Beloved Father and Friend. June 12th, 1965—June 22nd, 2009.

I looked up to Old, who was still holding my hand. "Is it weird if I talk?"

He shook his head. "Not at all. Do whatever you need to."

Without me asking him, he took a few steps back to give me and my father some privacy. Going far enough to be out of earshot but still visibly close enough to let me know he was here.

"Dad…"

Immediately, my heart cracked open, and tears uncontrollably trespassed the barrier of my eyelids. My mind flooded with thoughts and memories of my father, realizing that even though our time was short, it was full.

"Dad…I need you. I feel like I'm drowning underneath the weight of so much pain. And if I'm being honest, sometimes that pain feels like anger. And…I guess I blamed you for a lot of that pain and anger. I feel abandoned. I feel alone…and all of these feelings are just exhausting."

I paused for what felt like fifteen minutes. As I stood there in silence with more tears streaming down my face, a peace and strength that I just cannot explain surrounded me. I pulled out my phone and opened my text message thread with Zaire. Scrolling past the memes and pictures we would send each other, I went to a verse I remember he sent me a few days ago.

Psalm 27:10 (NLT), "Even if my father and mother abandon me, the Lord will hold me close."

I immediately FaceTimed him for him to break down the verse and explained that even though my parents didn't abandon me in a typical sense, I still had a very real and very loving Father.

I took a deep breath and started again.

"Dad, I need you. There's still so much about You that I don't understand, but I believe that I can trust You. I believe that You love me and always have. I believe that You died for me and rose again. I know I've done a lot that probably isn't pleasing to You, but I ask that You forgive me. If You would, please take away all this pain and live inside of me. I accept You. And I'll do my best to live a life that pleases You." I stood there silent for a moment, drying my face with my fingers and smiling like a little girl.

ALL THINGS BEAUTIFUL

In church, I learned that accepting Christ was choosing to die to myself and live in the spirit. How coincidental that I would die here, at a memorial.

I turned around and walked towards Zaire. He jogged towards me and met me halfway. He again placed his hands on the sides of my face and searched my eyes, ensuring I was okay. Content with whatever he saw, he held my hand and led me towards his car.

"Guess what?" I said, sounding giddy with excitement.

He stopped in his tracks and looked at me. "What is it?"

"I said goodbye to my father…and hello to the Father." I laughed by myself at my own corny joke.

Zaire's eyebrows arched with confusion.

I let out a sigh. "Ugh. That was a good one, too. But I accepted Christ…just now."

He smiled ear to ear, wrapped both of his arms around my neck, and hugged me. I smiled to myself and I wiped from my face fresh tears. Still holding onto me, he cheered and shouted various expressions of "glory, hallelujah!" causing a few passersby to take notice. Not caring, I joined in also shouting hallelujah, thanking God for accepting me, immediately noticing that this moment here with my Father and my new brother was also full.

CHAPTER 16

"And then what happened?"

"And then Missy made a big mess with the crayons and started crying," Hope informed.

"And then Ms. Cammie put everyone in a time-out. Even us, Daddy," Grace cleared up.

"Did you girls help Ms. Cammie clean up?"

"I did during nap time, Daddy," Hope chimed in.

"What about you, Grace?"

"I didn't help..." Grace sniffled. "I took a nap. I'm sorry."

"It's okay, Gracey. Just make sure you both apologize tomorrow. It doesn't matter what everyone else is doing; you both know better, and I expect you to do better."

"Okay, Daddy."

I looked in the mirror and watched as both girls nodded their heads. I always asked Ms. Cammie how the school day went. She knew I was also a teacher at the school, and even though I had never worked with children under the age of eleven, I knew how rambunctious the younger ones could get. Today, to my surprise, both of the girls had red faces on their daily report sheets.

I pulled my car into the drive-through lane at Chick-fil-A, and immediately, both girls perked up, calling out what they didn't want, the same thing every single time.

After placing the orders and driving up to the window, my phone chimed with Zipporah's face on my car panel.

"Hey, beautiful. How are you?"

My girls giggled to themselves in the backseat.

"Hey, my love." I could hear her smiling on the other end. "I'm well. The shoot is going a little longer than I planned, and I just wanted to give you the heads up."

"Okay. No problem."

I picked up the food and calmed my girls down, reminding them that they would eat once we got home. I had learned my mistake from finding fries, chicken nuggets, and other old, crumpled-up pieces of food lodged in their seats.

"Do you need me to help you out with anything or grab something for you?"

"Uhhh…. If you don't mind picking Peyton up from home, that'd be great. That way, once I'm finished with the shoot, I can just head your way."

"Okay, got it."

I was already a few minutes from home, but I really didn't mind. I made a giant U-turn and headed back to pick up her daughter. It was the Wednesday before Thanksgiving, and we made plans to spend the remainder of the week together with our children. I didn't know what time the shoot would end and didn't want to risk her deciding she was too tired and much rather fall asleep in her own bed.

"Thank you. Thank you."

"No problem, beautiful. I love you. See you later."

Again, I could hear her smiling. "I love you, too."

***

I had to admit to myself I was a little nervous about being with Peyton one-on-one. This weekend was important to me for several reasons. It wasn't about the holiday or the extended sleepover for that matter; this was the first time with us all together as a family since the Harvest Fest. I needed to solidify to myself, to my daughters, and to both Zipporah and Peyton that we could work as a family.

I got out of my car, leaving both girls still strapped in the backseat, and knocked on the front door.

"Hey, Mr. Timothy! Happy Thanksgiving Eve!" Peyton sang after opening the door. She sounded much more peppery than she had with me before.

If this was the tone for the weekend, I was in luck.

She started making struggling noises, and I poked my head in to find her trying to haul three suitcases all on her own.

"Hey, I can get these. You can go sit in the car with the girls."

She didn't hesitate or offer a rebuttal. She thanked me and walked to my car. One by one, I loaded the packed bags into the trunk. If four days between two women meant three fully packed suitcases, not including the duffle bag Peyton had in her lap, I was in for an adventure when they both eventually moved in. Assuming everything went smoothly.

The car ride was friendly enough. Hope and Grace kept her thoroughly entertained with all of their questions. I loved that Peyton addressed them as individuals and answered all of their questions. I could tell my girls looked up to her, and it was nice to see their relationship dynamic in person. They laughed and exchanged stories for the majority of the car ride.

We engaged in some small talk, where she informed me that she was looking forward to Christmas break, where she would be going back to California to spend time with her father and her cousins, Stephanie and Stirling.

"Are you all the same age?"

"Nope. Stirling is two years older, and Stephanie is two

years younger. We're a sandwich." She laughed at her own joke. My girls joined in on the laughter, even though I'm sure they didn't understand, and I laughed because this was much better than the silent drive I'd expected.

After thirty more minutes stuck in the city traffic, I pulled into the driveway of my home. I unbuckled Hope's car seat and held her hand as she jumped out of the car. Instead of walking over to get Grace, as I typically did, Peyton unbuckled her seat.

I typed in the code to the keypad at the front door and made a mental note that I needed to text Zipporah the code just in case she walked in really late. Scratch that; I needed to make her a code she would remember.

Both girls ran in with their bag of Chick-fil-A and threw off their backpacks by the front door. Peyton slowly entered as if she was still unsure about something.

"Don't forget to wash your hands and pray before you eat," I called out after the girls, who were now halfway up the stairs.

I turned on a few of the lights and started giving Peyton a tour.

"Well, this is the kitchen...I guess that's obvious." I walked over to the cabinets. "Feel free to help yourself to anything any time. I'm not typically a snacker, but I did pick up some things for you and Z."

"Do you have popcorn and M&Ms?"

"Yes, ma'am." I was suddenly glad I made a trip to the grocery store and picked up recurring items I'd seen Zipporah eat or mention.

"Awesome sauce. I'll keep that in mind for my midnight snack." She laughed, tapping at her temple.

I continued on with the tour, showing her room after room. After a while, it seemed a bit ridiculous to have this much space for a single guy with two small daughters who preferred to sleep in the same bed instead of their individuals.

"This is the basement. I honestly never really go in there. When I purchased this home with Melissa..." I looked at Peyton, not sure if she knew who Melissa was, but since she didn't flinch or ask any questions, I assumed she knew. "When I purchased this home with Melissa, I had plans to turn this into a man cave. That, as you can see, never happened."

I watched as she walked around, touching the bare walls.

"This is huge. I think our entire condo could fit down here."

"Do you think your mom would like it?"

Her neck snapped towards me. "To live? Down here?"

I laughed, "No. For a studio. She's been complaining recently about not having enough space. I'm sure she's only going to get more clients after the magazine comes out. I've never done anything with it. It might as well go to her."

She nodded her head in agreement. "I can see that. Yeah, I think she'll like it."

For the remainder of the tour, Peyton wasn't as peppery as she was earlier. I wasn't sure what had changed, but something about her mood was off since she left the basement.

We ended the tour upstairs in the room that she would be spending the week in. I had considered this for a long time. There were only two master bedrooms in my home, and one, the one on the main floor, was where I hoped Zipporah would eventually join me. I had full plans for the girls to eventually take this room, with them being my first children. The only reason they weren't in it now is because Nicole stayed in here for weeks after Melissa passed. Even when she got around to getting her own place, I never switched the girls' room. Now, with the mural Zipporah had painted, it didn't feel right moving them.

Peyton wasn't my biological child, but she was the oldest child nonetheless. The room had a window, a walk-in closet, and a private bathroom. I wanted her to be comfortable here and to know that my plans for the future include both Zipporah and her.

"And this is your room. Well, where you're sleeping this weekend. But…also your room. If you like it."

"Really?" she asked, with a hint of disbelief.

"Yeah." I lowered my voice to a whisper, "I told you about my plans with your mom…and those plans include you. So, if you want it, it's yours."

"Wow." Peyton walked into the room and twirled around. "This is nice, Mr. Timothy. Thanks."

I nodded my head and left her to her thoughts. I jogged down the stairs and, one by one, unloaded a suitcase, brought it upstairs, and repeated that cycle. I would definitely need additional help when they moved in. Once finished, I gave Hope and Grace a bath and let them pick out their pajamas. Typically, I preferred for them to be in bed by 7:30, but they pleaded with me to stay up and watch a movie with Peyton. I gave them the okay as long as she was okay with it. She came out of her room, already changed into her pajamas.

We sat on the couch, and I scrolled through the children and family categories on a few different subscription apps until we landed on a movie that I was sure would bore me to death. I clicked play and heard the noises of someone attempting to put their code in the lock. I walked over to the door and checked the peephole before opening it up wide with open arms, ready to receive her.

She smiled. "Hey. I missed you." She leaned into me and wrapped her arms around my neck. I secured both of my arms around her waist and carried her over the threshold, locking the door behind us.

"You look...wow." Zipporah was always beautiful without trying. Her hair was slicked into a low bun, her makeup looked ethereal with gold flecks on her cheeks, neck, and hair. Her lips were slightly red, as if she had lipstick on but it wore off throughout the day.

"Mommy!" Peyton yelled from the living room, and quick footsteps could be heard, followed by a set of two smaller footsteps.

I set her down, and she high-fived her daughter with both hands and kissed her on the cheek.

"Hey, Sweet P. I missed you so much. If I ever have to do something like this again, you're ditching school and coming with me."

"You look like a rockstar, Mom." Peyton sounded in awe, touching the gold foil on her mom's right cheek that trailed down her neck.

"Thanks, dude! I'm exhausted, but it was still a lot of fun."

She squatted down and hugged each of my girls one by one, allowing them to run their hands over the gold foil on her face and hair.

"Ms. Z, did you take the pictures today?" Hope asked.

She nodded her head. "Mm-hm. I did." She removed a crumpled piece of paper from her pocket and opened it up, pressing a piece of gold foil on their cheeks. She then handed the piece of paper to Peyton, giving her a wink.

"I told you I'd bring you something back."

"Thanks, Mommy." Peyton folded the paper and ran upstairs to her room.

She threw off her shoes and removed her coat, throwing it on the rack by the door. She held the hand of Grace and Hope in one of hers and walked towards the living room.

"You started a movie without me? Traitor!" She laughed, and both of my girls followed suit.

Peyton came down the stairs and joined her mom on the couch, rambling on about something.

If this is what I had to look forward to, this was perfect.

***

I tossed and turned for what felt like the hundredth time tonight. This part was not perfect. While Zipporah took my bed to herself, I slept on the couch in the living room.

She objected, but I knew I couldn't sleep with her on my bed and not struggle to keep my hands to myself. She offered to sleep on the couch next to me, but she had a long day, and from the soft snores I heard coming from the bedroom, I'd made the right choice.

Yes, I still have two empty rooms upstairs, but I preferred to be downstairs, closer to all the entrances and exits.

I got up, frustrated with my couch, and dragged my libs upstairs to check on Hope and Grace. They were both sound asleep. How? I'm not sure because Grace's legs were on Hope's stomach, and Hope's legs were sliding off the bed. I rearranged them and quietly walked out of the room, closing the door behind me. When I turned around, I found Peyton trying to sneak down the steps, holding what looked like the sheets on her bed.

"Hey, Peyton. Is everything okay? Do you need something?"

She stopped in place and tried to hide her face behind the sheets. "I need my mom. Is she sleeping?"

"It sounded like she was. Is there something I can help you with?"

Even behind the sheets, I could see her shoulders drop. She let out a deep sigh. "I need to put these in your washing machine."

"Oh. Don't worry about it. Let me take these. The laundry room is behind the kitchen." I grabbed the soiled sheets, and we walked into the laundry room.

ALL THINGS BEAUTIFUL

After starting the load, I washed my hands, not sure what to say because it was obvious she was embarrassed, and I didn't want to make anything worse at a failed attempt to try and soothe her.

I grabbed a set of extra sheets, and she followed me upstairs to her room. I laid the sheets on the dresser when I realized the mattress still needed to dry.

"I'm really sorry. I didn't mean to...at home, my mom puts these cotton pads underneath the sheets. Just in case."

I nodded. "It's cool. I'll order them on Amazon. Hopefully, they can get in tomorrow. I wish my mom knew about cotton pads when I was younger."

Her eyes opened wide. "Did you...did you also have accidents?"

"I did." I scruffed my face with my hands. "For a really long time," I admitted. "Eventually, I just got over it and started waking up. Not sure what clicked in my brain, but something did. And I stopped having all those dreams that I was in a bathroom and was free to relieve myself."

"Oh my gosh!" she roared. "I thought that was just me! I'll be doing something completely unrelated and then a random toilet just appears."

"At least you have your mom. My brother teased me about it every day. I'm pretty sure that only made it worse." I often responded by reminding him he was high as a giraffe's belly button, but left that part out.

I got a mobile fan from the garage and set it up so it would blow over the side of the bed that was wet. She showered and changed into a new set of PJs.

"Are you going back to bed?"

I turned around. "I'm going to try. My couch is not nearly as soft as the one in your house."

"Do you want a snack?"

"Sure."

On our way towards the kitchen, she asked, "Do you have almond butter?"

"Yup." I removed all of the chunky peanut butter when her mom told me she was allergic. Well, after I inhaled two giant spoonfuls of it myself.

She got four slices of bread, coated each slice with almond butter, and sprinkled cinnamon on top.

"Do you have Oreos?"

"Uhhh…" I wasn't sure where this was going. I pointed to a cabinet that I believed still had the treat.

She rummaged through the pantry and found a small bag of mini Oreos. "Perfect! Okay, you're going to have to just trust me. I know what I'm doing when it comes to snacks." She crushed the bag of Oreos with her hands and then sprinkled them on one slice of the bread before closing the sandwich and handing me one.

I looked at it suspiciously.

"Just try it. You at least have to try it," she rationalized.

I opened my mouth and ate a piece of the sandwich. It wasn't my favorite, not that it wasn't good, because somehow the flavors did work, but I wasn't a big sweets guy. I prefer my peanut butter sandwiches, just chunky PB, no jelly.

"It's not bad, I'll give you that."

"Told you." She stuffed a piece of her sandwich into her mouth. "So…Mr. Timothy. Tell me more about your plans to marry my mom."

CHAPTER 17

"Happy Thanksgiving." I hugged Mrs. Charlise and then Mr. Williams. "I'm so glad I was able to meet you both.

"Happy Thanksgiving! It was truly a pleasure." Charlise smiled, dabbing the corner of her eyes.

William nodded in agreement and wrapped an arm around his wife.

"Bye, Daddy!" Nicole hopped up and kissed her father on the cheek. "Bye, Momma. I'll see you both soon. And Momma, stop crying. This is a good thing."

"No, it is a good thing," Charlise declared. "A really good thing. It makes me a little sad because it reminds me that my baby is gone…but I am so happy for you, Zaire. And for both of those little girls."

Zaire wrapped both of his arms around Charlise and hugged her. "I know, Momma. I know. It can be a sad thing and a good thing at the same time."

Even though he couldn't see me, I nodded my head in agreement. Zaire walked his mother and father-in-law out to their car.

Nicole linked her arm with mine, and we started walking towards the dining room table. "I'm sorry about my mom; she can be a bit dramatic."

"Ohh. So that's where you get it from," I jested. "No, it's okay. She was really sweet, and I do get it. All things considered."

I spent the morning helping Mrs. Joyce, Daisha, and Nicole in the kitchen. I wasn't anything close to a chef, but it was nice being a part of their family tradition. We whispered and laughed to ourselves, sharing stories about the men in our lives. It was nice and something I'd never participated in before. I looked forward to making many more memories with these women and in this kitchen.

I was really surprised to meet Charlise and William. I didn't really know what to expect from the parents of Zaire's late wife. Charlise had taut sienna skin, and her hair was a mix of black and gray waist-length locs. William was handsome. His skin was bright and fair, much like Nicole's, but his hair was red, like Melissa's. Both of them were welcoming and equally excited to meet me and my daughter.

Speaking of Peyton, she spent half of the morning giving both Hope and Grace the cutest hairstyle of three ponytails that ended in twists. They were beyond excited for a hairstyle that seemed so simple. Even Zaire was stunned and grateful. I was just happy that we were working, or blending, as Peyton called it.

While in the backyard, I helped to prepare everything for Eden and Daisha's pregnancy/gender reveal. I offered to handle it alone instead so that both Daisha and Nicole would be surprised. I made sure to wash my hands well to keep from accidentally spoiling the news. I walked inside and found Nicole on the floor, playing spoons with Peyton.

"It's all ready," I whispered to Nicole. She nodded and got up from the floor.

"Okay, everyone, if you all will follow me outside, please," Nicole instructed.

Without too much fuss, everyone gathered outside and made way for Daisha and Eden to take center stage, now both wearing matching white shirts and jeans.

"What's going on?" Mrs. Joyce asked.

"Yeah, it's cold out here, Nicky. Will we be out here long?" Mr. Robert asked, wrapping his arms around his wife.

"Well…we won't be out here long. But Daisha and I wanted to tell you all together that…" Eden looked at Daisha and smiled.

"We're pregnant!" They shouted together in unison.

"They are?" Peyton asked me.

I nodded my head yes, and she smiled and cheered along with the rest of the small crowd.

"We've known for quite a while now but wanted to wait and tell you so that together we could find out what we're having."

I took my queue and brought them each a popper that I filled with chalk dust the color signifying the sex of their baby.

"Thanks, sis." Eden smiled.

"No problem." I smiled.

Eden and I clicked almost as quickly as I did with Nicole. He made it a point to call me sis and said he could tell I was here to stay. I enjoyed watching Zaire turn into a goofball with his brother. They jabbed and jested each other often, but you knew there was serious love between the two of them. The fact that he was a counselor thrilled Peyton. They spent much of their conversations talking about everything from eating to dissociative disorders.

I stepped back and stood next to Peyton, who was standing next to Zaire. Zaire wrapped an arm around me and kissed my cheek.

They shook the poppers and counted down, with us joining in.

"Three…two…one."

They pushed the end, and a cloud of pink surrounded them, covering their shirts. They hugged and rocked each other while Eden loudly hollered and whooped.

"Let's gooo!" Eden shouted.

"Congratulations, bro. I'm happy for you." Zaire clapped hands with and then hugged his brother.

"You're next, man. Trust me," Eden thought he whispered.

After taking turns congratulating the couple, we walked back inside to get out of the cold. Eden and Daisha were both covered in pink but didn't seem to care. Nicole went back to playing cards with Peyton. Zaire's parents were holding his girls and making sure they didn't stick their fingers into any more pies.

I sat on Zaire's lap and rested my head against his shoulder.

"You know what I'm thankful for this year?"

"Tell me."

"I'm thankful for all of you. You've made me feel welcomed, and I know Peyton feels that way, too. I didn't grow up with all of this, and I'm really glad to have you all in my life now and in hers. In all of my childhood memories, there were just me and my dad. I'm glad she has grandparents, her dad, cousins, and now you, sisters, aunties, uncles, and a soon-to-be niece."

"That sounds like we're all a family." He interlocked his fingers with mine.

"We are a family, a big mixed your kids, my kid, maybe someday our kids, family."

"Would you like all of that with me?"

"Mmm…" I took a long pause like I haven't considered what our future would look like together a million times over. "With you, Old, I want everything. No more distance and cities. No more years apart. Just this one. Us and our family. Forever."

***

"We at 'Creative And' are so happy to honor this year's selection of black and brown artists. Please enjoy yourselves this evening as well as the exhibit. You deserve it."

Claps and shouts of appraisal were dispersed throughout the small crowd. Audrey and her team held a small congratulatory party at the gallery for each of the twelve artists being honored and reviewed in the winter edit. We were each only able to bring one guest, and as badly as I wanted Peyton to be here, I knew I had to share this moment with Zaire.

Peyton seemed happy enough to stay behind and

babysit H and G. Neither of them was able to distract her enough from making sure my curls were perfect, doing my makeup, and forcing me into this skin-tight, champagne-colored gown.

She even helped Zaire prep by giving him a full facial. He texted me with several emojis, saying "he was in there." Not to mention making sure he wore the right color tie and handkerchief to match my dress.

"Ready?" I looked at Zaire, who was still looking at me all doe-eyed like he had been since after Thanksgiving.

"After you."

I held his hand and dragged him as quickly as I could in my heels, which I was beginning to regret. I was a stickler about him not looking at any of the unfinished pieces for this specific exhibit. I wanted him to be surprised because he, after all, helped inspire it.

We passed several other artist corners until we reached mine.

"Do you like it?"

"I do. It feels…raw? I don't know if I'm explaining it right at all. Maybe you should explain it to me."

"No…no. Go with it. Tell me how it makes *you* feel."

He looked at me and huffed. "Okay…I'm going to try not to embarrass myself. It feels raw, not in an undercooked way…"

I stifled a laugh behind my hand.

He glared at me, and I smiled, encouraging him to continue.

"But in an exposed way. I guess? It feels intense and sad…really sad?"

"Wow. You did really well, my love."

I painted the most obscure and abstract piece I had ever painted. It was the same painting I had been working on in my idle time from a few months ago. In the center was a gaping black hole, and all around were spirals of splotches of colors. In some areas the black spilled into the colors more than others. Regardless of which emphasized more, there was always both.

He bent his neck and read the gold-plastered inscription card near a quick bio of me as the artist and read, "'The Ambivalence of Time' created by Zipporah Smith, 2023. If you allow yourself, all you'll see is black, and that can consume you and leave you empty and wanting. Still, if you allow yourself, there can be much love from pain, joy from mourning, and laughter from sadness. All things can be beautiful within its time.'"

He looked at me with a jovial grin that started at his mouth and reached his eyes. "I am so proud of you."

"Thank you." I beamed. "I'm proud of myself, too."

We made our way through the party, engaging with the other artists and their guests. Before long, my legs started to ache, and I considered hoisting up my dress and removing my heels.

I anchored myself to Zaire's side to relieve some of the pressure off the balls of my feet.

"Are you ready to go?" he whispered in my ear.

"Yes, please! I need to get out of this immediately."

We both stifled laughs and quietly made our escape. I was grateful for Audrey and all the eyes I was sure the edit would bring to my work, but I was ready to go home. *Home.*

"Do you want to move in together?"

Zaire looked at me, confused, briefly before focusing on the road. "What are you talking about?"

I hesitated briefly, not sure why his answer wasn't a resounding yes. "I'm thinking about how badly I can't wait to get home and I can no longer tell the difference between my home, home, and your home, home. So, why not cut the fluff and move in together? And yes, maybe that's a bit unconventional. And I know we still have our boundaries, but with all of our kids there, I'm sure we won't…"

He rubbed the back of my hand and laughed. "I get

what you mean. Can we talk about this later?"

I nodded, but on the inside, I was stirring. I didn't get time to process if my feelings were hurt or if I was just angry because we arrived at his home. We walked into his home, which was eerily quiet, for all three of our children to be there.

"Did Nicole end up coming over?" I asked, wondering if she'd maybe taken them out for pizza.

"Actually, everyone is down in the basement. We have something we want to show you."

"Mmm…. So, I'm finally going to see what everyone has been whispering about? Okay, cool."

He laughed and helped me down the stairs. When we arrived at his basement, it wasn't the blank, stark white walls that it once was. There were canvases and piles of clay, a spinning wheel, tools, easels, and all of the fixings that would be needed for a studio. The lighting was no longer harsh and unpleasant but dimmed and moody. A few windows had been installed so you could see the night sky.

"So *this* is what you've been working on?"

Before he could respond, the sound of feet rushing down the stairs echoed in the basement, with Peyton, Hope, and Grace soon following, all of them in similar champagne-colored dresses.

PATRICE JOSEPH

I pointed a finger at Peyton, who, up until this point, had never kept a secret from me. She just smiled in response.

Grace and Hope started clapping their hands and shouting, "Yay, Daddy!"

I turned around. "Old? What?" For the first time in maybe my entire life, I was lost for words.

Zaire bent down and got on one knee. I could hear Peyton squeal behind me.

"Zipporah, this moment right here in front of you feels like *déjà vu* to me, and I take that to mean that I'm exactly where the Lord would have me to be. All I want for the rest of my life is for you to be with me. You asked me just now if we could move in together, but you've already moved in. I made space for you in my heart and my mind, and you have taken up all that space with your laughter and your beauty." He motioned with his fingers for Grace and Hope to stand beside him, and they did. "Would you and Peyton both be our family? And will you be my wife?"

Peyton walked over to him, handed him a small silver box, and gave him a hug. He hugged her back, and now, when he looked at me, he had tears in his eyes.

I'm not sure what made me the most emotional, whether it was the look of his two little girls looking at me in complete awe, awaiting my answer, or if it was him, this man that I once thought I made up in a dream, or my daughter here beside him smiling, giving me two thumbs up.

"*Yes!*" I didn't mean to sound eager, but I have thought about Old almost every day for the past fifteen years. I was eager for our lives to finally move forward together.

He opened up the box and revealed a striking pear-cut, emerald-colored engagement ring with a twisted, almost vine-like gold band. I didn't know what to expect. I had braced myself for whatever gaudy piece of fine jewelry he had picked out. But this was unique; it wasn't presumptuous. It was different; it was me.

"Woah."

He smiled with a lifted chest. "Do you like it?"

"I do. I actually do."

EPILOGUE

Winter

"Isn't it a thing that I'm not supposed to see you before the wedding?" I rubbed my eyes, looked at the bright screen, and waited for my eyes to focus on the time. It was 7:03 a.m., and according to the schedule Peyton and Nicole created, I still had two hours of sleep.

Zipporah and I didn't care much for weddings, but Peyton and Nicole took it upon themselves to do something "small" to celebrate our union. Peyton said if weddings were in the Bible, we needed to have a wedding, and she had proven to be a stickler when it came to all the details, ensuring this day would be without flaw.

"Don't tell me you're superstitious now, Mr. Timothy," Zipporah roared into the phone.

I laughed. "I'm not. I'm just sleepy." I let out a sigh and dragged my limbs out of the bed. "I'm up now. What do you need from me, Mrs. Timothy?"

"It might sound crazy if I tell you now. So just come and get me. Oh, and dress warm and bring lots of blankets. And can you also bring me my black coat?"

ALL THINGS BEAUTIFUL

I rubbed my eyes with the back of my hands and nodded as if she could see me. "Okay, beautiful. I'll let you know when I'm outside. If Nicole catches you trying to sneak out the day of the wedding, it's on you."

She laughed, and we hung up the phone.

I did my morning rituals, said a prayer, packed what the Mrs. wanted, and headed her way. Zipporah, Peyton, Hope, and Grace spent the night at Nicole's and would get ready there today. I spent the night alone in my home, and although I wasn't a morning person and would now be lying in bed with someone who considered sleep optional, I missed them and was glad last night was the last night I wouldn't be without them again.

I hurried over to Nicole's home and found a U-Haul truck with a young couple unloading their things into Zipporah's old home. She listed it for sale shortly after our engagement, and thankfully, it wasn't on the market long. I walked up to the front door and said a prayer over the new neighbors.

Zipporah opened after a few knocks and kissed me immediately.

"Good morning, husband."

God, I love this woman.

"Good morning, wife. Where would you have me take you this morning on this very impromptu wedding day adventure?"

"To Eden's house. I need the pool."

Eden and Daisha had finally purchased a home in the northern Marietta area. While they were still getting used to it, I think they were both glad to have one place to call home.

I shook my head, unsure of exactly what my wife was suggesting but relenting to her wishes as I would gladly do for the rest of my life.

We arrived at their home at 8 a.m. on the dot.

"Okay, whatever you're doing, we better make it fast. I do not want to get on Peyton's bad side."

"I texted Daisha to let her know we'd be here. I think this will be quick."

I followed her out of the car, quietly through their home, and into the backyard.

"I want you to baptize me. And I want it to be today. It has to be today, and I want you to do it," Zipporah proclaimed.

Understanding the assignment, I wish I had dressed a little warmer. The topic of baptism had been a recurring one in our home the past few days. While she, like many others, thought it should be done when someone is a little further down their walk and more "experienced," I explained how baptism is a physical declaration of something that has happened inward. We studied scriptures together about baptism, and she said she would think about it.

"What changed your mind? Why today?"

She shrugged. "I've been thinking about it all night. And I just figured, if this wedding is happening to celebrate our love, I want to start the day off celebrating the best love of my life."

I nodded in agreement again. "Okay. I get it. Let's do it."

I got in the pool first and prayed, preparing to baptize my wife on our wedding day. I thought back to all the years I thought were lost and wasted, and now, in this moment, all I could feel was the faithfulness of God.

She shivered as she entered the pool.

"I've never done this before," I admitted to her. "Not exactly sure what to say."

"I've never done this before, either." She laughed, unphased by my inexperience.

I paused briefly and reminded myself that this wasn't about me or words but all about Jesus. We spent a moment together in quick prayer, and I baptized her. She came out of the water with a wide smile and a mix of water and tears trickling down her face.

I got out before her, held blankets in towels in my arms, and wrapped her in them once she got out of the pool.

"How do you feel?" I asked, wrapping myself now in a set of blankets and towels.

"Forgiven. Whole. Healed. New."

***

I walked down the aisle with my brother behind me. Once at the altar, I looked around at all the faces of the people here to support us. I'm glad we decided to do this in the backyard of our home instead of at a church.

I had done a church wedding before, and now, I was getting to experience something new with New.

The moment the song Zipporah chose for the processional began, I knew I had made the right choice. I would spend the rest of my life thanking Nicole and Peyton for forcing us to do this.

Peyton walked out first in a beautiful white satin gown. I smiled at her, and she smiled back, fist-bumping me before standing on the opposite side.

Next, Hope and Grace walked in together in white poofy tulle dresses, dropping a mixture of white and pink rose petals on the ground. The crowd gushed over both of them as they made their way to the front and took their seats.

The tempo of the music slowed and faded into a new song, and my heartbeat slowed with it. All of our near misses, should'ves, could'ves, and would'ves lead us to this very moment.

Then came my bride as the audience stood to their feet. She was breathtaking. Although I had seen her just earlier this morning, her hair was covered in a satin cap, and I had never seen her dress. All of her hair was swept up into a loose, curly updo, with a few tendrils curled and framing her face. Her face was "beat," as Peyton would say, but it wasn't heavy or cakey-looking. Her ivory dress was fitted to her body and accentuated her curves, cascading around her feet. She was golden. Even on this cold, cloudy day, her skin and her eyes were golden, charging everything with their warmth.

I couldn't take my eyes off of her.

"You look so handsome, my love," she said the moment she made it to the altar.

"You look…you look…"

She looked into the crowd, specifically at Nicole, and said loudly, "Take his breath away? Check!"

The crowd erupted in laughter. This was it. This was the rest of my life with her.

The minister from our church said all the things I believe he was supposed to say, but I barely heard a word.

I just kept looking at her and thanking God for His favor.

Zipporah, letting go of my hands, broke the chain of my thoughts as she reached into her bosom and retrieved her vows.

"Zaire." She paused for a moment, and I saw the glistening in her eyes. "Zaire, I don't know if you remember, but we met on this exact day years ago, when you and I were both twelve, on a ski lift."

I nodded my head because I did remember.

She continued, "I have loved you before I even knew what love meant."

I looked down and watched a single tear leave my eye and land on my brown shoe. I felt my brother's hand touch my shoulder. I composed myself quickly and faced her again.

"I know what love means now because of you, all the people you've brought into our lives, and because of our Father. I vow to always love you, to cherish every single moment, and to jump with you even when I'm scared." She looked back into the crowd. "Did you guys see that tear? Check!"

I howled along with her and the crowd.

After the crowd settled, I reached into my pocket and opened up the blank sheet of paper. Nicole hounded me to write my vows, but I told her I didn't have to. I knew exactly what I wanted to say.

"Zipporah. First, I do remember. And if memory serves me right, you dared me to get on that ski lift. We had just met, and what you call love, I remember as being utterly terrified, and I'm pretty sure I almost peed in my pants."

She bent over in laughter and fanned her face.

I rolled my shoulders back and put the blank paper back in my pocket so I could hold her hands. "Zipporah, to know you is to know that there is a creator, and He is God. I can't look into the gold specs in your eyes and not know that He also hung the stars. I can't hear your laughter and not know that He created the hum of the waves. I can't watch you smile as easily as you breathe and not know that not only is there a God, but that He loves me.

"I know how much I love *our* daughters, how I would do anything to protect them, and I know that's how wildly God loves you. I vow to spend my life earning you, keeping you, and holding your hand as we jump." I gave her the handkerchief from my pocket. "Still coming in handy 'till this day." We both smiled as she dried her eyes.

I reached into my opposite pocket and pulled out a silver bracelet with a link silver and gold pendant.

"Peyton." I looked over New's shoulder into her wide, unexpecting eyes. "You matter to me. I promise to be here for you however you want me to be, and however you need me to be. I promise to support you and love you always."

I linked the bracelet around her small wrist, and she hugged me, causing more "awes" to gush from the crowd.

I knew my girls, so I fully expected them to rush to the altar like they did, expecting their jewelry. I kissed both of their cheeks and gave them smaller versions of Peyton's bracelet.

I stood in front of my wife again and held her hands.

"Thank you," she whispered.

I just smiled. She didn't need to thank me. I meant my promises and vows to both of them.

The minister continued with the ceremony and pronounced us officially, husband and wife. I kissed my wife and scooped her into my arms as our family clapped, hoorayed, and threw confetti.

Nicole walked towards us. "All right. It's cocktail hour, and then we'll do the first dance, okay?"

I brushed past Nicole and nodded my head, still carrying my wife.

"Z, just one hour, okay?" she yelled behind us.

"Is one hour good for you?" I asked, looking down at her face.

She winked deviously. "We gave them the wedding they wanted; our honeymoon starts now."

Spring

"What does it say, Mommy?" Hope held both of her hands in a prayer position. She told me she was praying really long and hard for a baby brother or sister.

"Mommy, how many more minutes?" Grace asked impatiently. She had made it clear that she wanted a baby brother and not a sister.

"Four more minutes." I held out four fingers.

"We might as well just start picking out names…just in case, right, Z?" Peyton asked, looking over my shoulder and waiting for the results to appear.

In our short time since moving in together and becoming a family, we had blended together really well. I never expected either of Zaire's daughters to refer to me as "Mommy." I was content being Ms. Z forever and ever, but one day, it just happened. Zaire encouraged me to go with it as long as I felt comfortable. I already considered them to be mine and was honored for them to extend that title to me.

Zaire teared up when Peyton stopped calling him Mr. Timothy and started referring to him as Z. He let her paint his toes, tweeze his eyebrows, curl his hair, and do whatever else she wanted to experiment on him. I was just happy to not always be the test dummy for her "treatments." They built their own special and unique bond outside of me.

Zaire rubbed his hands together. "I don't think it could hurt. I'm pretty sure your mom is pregnant."

"What is that supposed to mean?" I shifted my weight over to my other foot, waiting for Zaire to respond.

"Nothing bad, beautiful. Me and Jesus like this. I know you're pregnant," he said while twisting his middle finger over his index.

"Okay, what do you think…*if* it's a girl," I said, tickling Hope and Grace.

They both laughed, and Gracey pouted after regaining her composure. She did not want to hear anything about another little girl.

"If it's a girl, let's name her…" Hope tapped on her chin. "Isabella!"

"Isabella?" Peyton and Zaire asked in unison.

I shook my head. "Not Isabella, Hopey."

"Any ideas, Peyton?" Zaire asked.

"Mm…. If it's a girl, I've always liked the name Skylar. Or Sky for short."

"Skylar," Zaire said out loud, testing how it sounded.

I wrinkled my nose. "Mmm. I don't know." I pointed my finger at Zaire. "You should name them. This was all your doing."

Zaire laughed. "Hey, man! I did not do this on my own. That is not what I remember at all."

"Please. Please, stop!" Peyton yelled, covering her ears.

Grace and Hope both joined in, covering their ears and saying, "Gross!"

I laughed and kissed Zaire on his cheek.

"Mom! Look!" Peyton shrieked in excitement.

I looked down at the test and covered my mouth, holding it up for Zaire.

"Mommy's pregnant, girls," Zaire announced.

He wrapped his arms around my hips, lifted my shirt, and placed several kisses on my stomach.

Both Grace and Hope lifted up their hands and I crouched a little to allow them to feel, even though I knew they wouldn't feel anything.

"We don't have a name for our brother yet," Grace announced.

"Not yet…but something will come to us," Peyton

mentioned.

"I will say, I do think it's going to be a boy."

"What makes you say that?" Zaire asked me.

"Jesus and I, we like this," I teased, wrapping my middle around my index fingers. I rubbed my belly. "Yeah…. He's a boy."

"Adam! Let's name him Adam!" Peyton declared.

Zaire and I looked at each other before looking down at Hope and Grace.

"I like Adam," Zaire agreed.

"Adam like in the Bible," Hope sang with her hands in the air.

"Adam is going to be my baby brother, and then he's going to marry Eve! But wait, Daddy, who am I going to marry?" Grace asked, looking far too concerned.

"It doesn't work like that, baby girl." He lifted both of his girls, one in each arm, and exited the bathroom. "And you never have to get married."

I turned around to face Peyton. "What do you think, dude?"

She scrunched her face. "I wanted another sister…" She laughed. "But a brother might be cool, too."

ALL THINGS BEAUTIFUL

Summer—Three Years Later

"It's not me!" I raised my hands and declared.

"It's not me," Daisha also raised her hands in defense. "Eden got snipped after our angel baby. The focus is on other kids now."

Momma Joyce had us all over for Sunday dinner, a tradition we started together, and was currently interrogating us, trying to figure out which one of us was currently pregnant.

Eden and Daisha had one girl, which, as Zaire guessed, was the spitting image of Eden. She had a beautiful caramel complexion with brown ringlets for hair and freckles on both cheeks. Her name was Amora. After Amora, they got pregnant rather quickly but miscarried. It was too early to know the gender of the baby. Two years ago, they both decided to start fostering older children who were in the system. Daisha, being in the system from a young age, knew all too well what it could be like being in a home where the caretakers only wanted a check.

"You guys already know I'm pregnant. It's not like it's a secret at this point," Nicole declared, pointing to her round and protruding belly.

Nicole and Eddie were on again and off again while he was trying to maintain being here part-time and in

California part-time. Peyton eventually sat him down for one of her sessions and told him he needed to face his fears of commitment. I had no idea that Eddie was dealing with anxiety and a fear of rejection stemming from his childhood. With Peyton holding him accountable, he sought therapy and committed to both Atlanta and Nicole full-time. They were married a year ago.

"It's not me," I bent over and picked up Adam, who I was still trying to wean from his pacifier. "My hands are still full with this one. Boys are a handful. Three girls were a breeze. Throw one boy in the mix, and I promise every day something breaks or there's a new bruise that needs tending to."

The ladies laughed as I looked into the eyes of my cute little chubster. Adam was a carbon copy of his father but had my skin complexion and light brown hair. Even his eyes had the same hazel and green undertones as Zaire's. I kissed his fluffy cheeks multiple times and set him down to resume playing with his blocks.

"And I know it's not Peyton," I yelled over the counter, leading into the living room.

"What isn't me, Mom?" Peyton yelled back.

"Nothing, Sweet P." I laughed.

Peyton was now fourteen and had already filled out. She was still overdressed, dripping in pink and sass, and one of my favorite people. On more than one occasion, I caught Austin looking in her direction a little too long for comfort. As far as she knew, they were still just friends. She was still all about the books, which comforted both Zaire and Eddie. Austin would soon be going away to college, and even though I couldn't care less about how he looked at her, he turned out to be a stand-up guy, maintaining his grades and keeping up in therapy.

"Do you need anything? I'm still in a session with Paige." Peyton walked in with AirPods in her ear and her iPad pencil in hand.

"Nope. You're good." I nodded my head and watched as she went back to the couch and resumed her telephone conversation with Paige.

In the corner of my eye, I saw a set of pink sneakers and a set of purple sneakers rushing down the stairs.

"Mommy, will you please tell Hope to share with me? She's always touching my things, and then when she has her things, she won't share them with me!" Grace pouted, holding a pink game controller.

I looked at Hope, who was also pouting and had her arms crossed, wearing a purple headset and, in one hand, a purple controller.

"Well, Mommy, it's just that she doesn't take care of my things. When I use her stuff, I always put it back, and today, my controller was dead, and I didn't even use it yesterday!"

I looked at both of them. Grace and Hope were now eight years old, and it was as if the older they got, the more I could tell them apart. That also may be because of how well I knew them and loved them.

"Are you guys mad at your sister, or are you mad at the situation?"

"The situation," Grace said.

"My sister," Hope stated.

Grace was softer, very expressive, and in tune with her emotions. She possessed a naturally gentle demeanor, and I often wondered if she was like her mother in that way. Hope, on the other hand, was bold, strong-willed, and independent. Grace was a natural extrovert, even though she was the quieter of the two. Hope, while a natural leader, preferred to keep to herself or be with her sister when they weren't fighting.

I took a moment away from the other women to help them problem-solve. Although not perfect, I hoped I was helping to raise them to be independent thinkers. After a few minutes of allowing them to go back and forth, we reached a compromise, and they both ran back upstairs to finish whatever video game they were playing.

The voices of the men carried as they walked in from the backyard to the kitchen.

"All the women in the kitchen? That's never a good sign," Robert bellowed, walking into the kitchen grabbing a bottle of water for himself and Joyce.

"Your mom says she has a hunch that someone is pregnant, my love." I looked up at Zaire as he draped his arms around me, burying his face into my hair and inhaling.

"Did you tell her it's not us?" Zaire laughed. "Our hands are full at the moment."

"Well, I'm already spoken for," Eddie jested, standing next to Nicole.

"Unless God did another miracle in me…it's not us, either," Eden said, rocking a sleepy Amora.

"Unh-Unh. If she said there's another baby here, believe me, there's another baby," Robert said, looking at all of us.

Autumn—Ten Years Later

"I'm going to miss you so much, Z," Peyton said into my shoulder, still holding on to the necklace she made from the bracelet I gifted her long ago.

"I'm a call away. Always just a phone call away." I rubbed her back and held her until she had gathered herself and went to hug her mom for the fifth time today.

Peyton was twenty-four and the spitting image of

her mother. She finished both her first two degrees in psychology at home with us in Atlanta but decided to pursue her doctoral degree in the State of Tennessee.

Peyton was a daughter to me, just as much as Hope and Grace were. I was just as sad to see her go as her mother was, but understanding that she both wanted and needed to experience life on her own terms, without us a staircase away and without her siblings and cousins always pulling her in a direction. She was a godsend, just as much as Zipporah was.

As Nicole predicted, the years came when hairstyles for Grace and Hope were the least of my worries. They both kept me level-headed and took the lead in the areas where I simply lacked the insight. Before she made her decision, she asked me what it was like to move away from my family when I first moved to Atlanta, and my parents still lived in South Carolina. I explained to her that while it was a tough decision, it was one of the best I'd ever made. I could only hope she would continue to grow more into the woman I knew she wanted to be.

"Call me every day, Sweet P. Every day," her mother reminded her, still squeezing her tightly.

"I will, Mom. I promise."

"This is going to be a good thing for you, trust me. God has a plan for you here." With that, I prayed over Peyton's condo and over her as well. With one final group hug, we left her to venture off into her own becoming.

***

"Thank you, Nicky. This really means a lot to us." I held the phone and angled it so both Zipporah and I were shown on the FaceTime call.

"No worries, Z. You two have fun! Here, hold this, Eddie. Let me go find Adam so he can say bye."

Nicky handed the phone off to Eddie, and we all laughed at her calling after the three boys. Adam was our youngest at thirteen years old. Eddie and Nicole had two of their own, Forrest and Hunter, both age eleven.

My mom was right when she had a hunch about someone having another baby; no one expected that to mean Nicole was having twins.

The sound of running was heard, followed by a loud crash, and ended with Nicole yelling and Eddie rushing off into the action. Adam soon picked up the FaceTime call.

"Hey, Dad!" Adam croaked.

Adam was still growing into his voice and his body. At thirteen, he was already five-foot-five, and I was sure he would grow to be well over six feet. He was our most rambunctious child, but it was fun having a boy, I have to admit. His uncle and I encouraged him to try out for sports, and, at the moment, he had a fair interest in basketball, with plans to try out for the team in September. If I had it my way, he'd have been playing from six years old, but his true passion was in science, and my wife wanted us to nurture that. At least, it was for the time being.

Everyone said he looked like me, but when I looked at him, I saw my wife's entire face.

"Hey, AD! Is that you that broke something in Nicole's house?"

"No, Dad, it wasn't even me. That was Forrest, I think. Can I talk to mom, please?"

I shook my head and handed the phone to Zipporah, who was smiling and sticking her tongue out at me because she believed she was the favorite parent of all of our children.

"Hey, baby. I miss you already."

Adam and Zipporah continued their conversation for a few more minutes. I used my phone to add myself to the call along with my other three daughters.

"Hey, Daddy!" Hope and Grace sang in unison.

"Hey, Z!" Peyton chimed.

Hope and Grace took the opportunity to reveal to us their freshly redecorated dorm room. Hope and Grace grew up to lead very separate lives and surprised us when they decided to go to school and room together.

Hope, although quite the talented singer, like her mother, wanted to become a school teacher and was determined to end up in the district. If you asked me, she would end up either in politics or being a lawyer. Grace, who was a gifted dancer and musician, wasn't yet sure of what she wanted to do in school, but wanted the college experience nonetheless. She was barely a month into school and had changed her major twice already. I was sure she would land with both feet on the ground.

"We just wanted to tell you all that we love you so much before we leave. We'll be back in two weeks. You guys all be careful and call us if there are any emergencies. Any time."

"Okay, Dad."

"Got it, Daddy."

"Sounds good, Z."

"Okay, Dadio."

"And I wanted to tell you all that I'm so sad you guys are all grown up and so happy at who you all are turning out to be," Zipporah expressed.

She was right. There were a lot of years when having children that outnumbered the adults put us in the ringer, but now that they were all also adults and young adult-ish children, I was also thankful.

"Awe. Thanks, Mommy."

"Mommy, you turned into such a sap."

"Love you too, Mommy!"

"Thank you, Mommy."

I ended the call with my I love yous and a prayer, as I always did and as I always would for as long as I was able.

***

We got in line to board our seats after premier boarding was called.

"Hey, I have an idea."

I faced Zipporah. "What's the idea?"

"Let's not board together. Let's act like this is our first time meeting. It might be fun."

I shook my head and brought our bags back to a seat while she boarded alone. I would do anything to please her. Anything to keep a smile on her face.

I decided to wait until the last minute and board a few moments before the final call and really throw myself into character.

I loaded my bag and her carry-on into the overhead bin and took my seat next to hers.

"Hi, there. My name's Zaire." I stretched out my hand and held it open.

She smiled and shook mine. "Hey, you. My name is Zipporah. Will this be your first time going to Greece?"

I nodded. "First time. How about yourself?"

"It'll be my first time as well."

I gritted my teeth as the flight took off, as I always did.

"Is this your first time flying?" she asked.

"No, not my first time. But I have been told I'm afraid of heights."

"Well, I actually know a cure for nerves." She opened up her hand, and I placed mine in hers. After so many years, it didn't happen too often, but I felt a quick whir of electricity when we touched.

I smiled as she gasped and quickly broke character to kiss the back of her hand.

"So, what's the cure?"

"It's something my dad and I used to do." She paused briefly, I'm sure thinking of her dad. I stroked her hand, reminding her I was there. She continued, "Whatever is the occasion that brings you on a sixteen-hour flight? And first class, no less."

"Today is actually my birthday," I responded.

"Really? How crazy! It's my birthday, too!"

"It's actually not so crazy, I've heard." I laughed.

"Happy birthday, Zipporah."

"Happy birthday, Zaire."

Printed in the USA
CPSIA information can be obtained
at www.ICGtesting.com
LVHW020856131124
796433LV00009B/163